USBORNE

CU
BREAKER

Which path
will YOU take?

Designed by Reuben Barrance
Edited by Sam Taplin

With thanks to Kate Nolan, Tom Taplin, Lan Cook,
Darran Stobbart and Tom Mumbray for their careful play-testing.

First published in 2022 by Usborne Publishing Ltd, Usborne House,
83-85 Saffron Hill, London EC1N 8RT, England. usborne.com

Usborne Verlag, Usborne Publishing Ltd, Prüfeninger Str. 20, 93049
Regensburg, Deutschland, VK Nr. 17560

Cover illustration by Christopher Park

Inside illustrations by Tom Knight

Text, cover illustration and inside illustrations
© Usborne Publishing, 2022

A CIP catalogue record for this book is available from the British Library.

ISBN 978-1-801-31430-5 7645/1 JFMAM JASOND/22

Printed in China.

USBORNE
ADVENTURE GAMEBOOKS

CURSE
BREAKER

Simon Tudhope
Illustrated by Tom Knight

These are not easy times to be a guard in the city of Mirewick. Sleepwalkers roam the streets at night, and no one seems to know why. Down in the dungeons, wild rumours of a coming invasion are dismissed as the ravings of fools. But when you yourself are sentenced to death, you realise sinister forces are at work.

From this point onwards, you are in control of an epic adventure. Every choice is yours, and your survival depends upon the decisions you make. There are battles to fight and picture clues to unravel as you draw ever closer to one final, fateful choice.

One thing is for certain: as the mysteries of Mirewick are laid bare, you'll see things are worse than you could possibly have dreamt...

HOW TO PLAY

This book is split into numbered entries. At the end of most entries, you'll be presented with a choice about what to do next. When you've made your choice, turn to that entry. Your adventure begins at entry 1, but after this it will proceed in the order determined by your choices.

LOG BOOK

Turn to the end of these instruction pages to see your Log Book. This is where you'll keep track of all the relevant details of your quest. It's split into the six sections detailed below, and you'll need a pencil to keep them all up-to-date.

Life points

You start with 12 Life points, but lose points if you're hurt. If you drop to 0 you die, and the game ends. At various points you'll be able to heal yourself and regain lost Life points, but **you can never have more than 12 in total.** Each time you gain or lose Life points, update the number in your Log Book.

Abilities

You have four abilities: ATHLETICISM, SIXTH SENSE, ENDURANCE and SKILL. Your starting level for each is 3 points. **Before you start the game, add 1 point to the ability of your choice.** At various moments in your quest, you will gain more Ability points. It's up to you which abilities to upgrade. If you receive more than 1 Ability point at the same time, you can add them all to the same ability, or spread them across different abilities. You can also lose Ability points, and you must decide which ability to downgrade. Remember to update your Log Book whenever an ability level changes.

Money

You don't start with any money, but you'll pick some up as your adventure progresses. The currency is shillings. Whenever you pick up or spend any money, remember to update the total number of shillings in your Log Book. You can only buy an item if you have enough money.

Items

You will both pick up and lose items on your adventure. Remember to write down any item that you pick up in your Log Book, and delete it if you're instructed to do so. Most items can help you in some way.

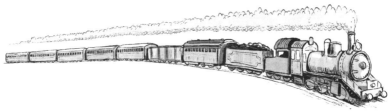

Notes

During your quest, you'll see and learn things that could be useful later on. It might be a small detail, or the entry number for a passage you want to refer back to. Whatever it is, you can jot it down in the notes section of your Log Book.

COMBAT

You fight by rolling two dice. Here's an example of what you'll see before combat starts:

GUARD

Rounds: 5   Damage: 2

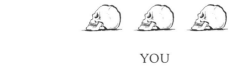

YOU

♡ ♡ ♡ ♡ ♡ ♡ ♡ ♡ ♡ ♡ ♡ ♡

The skulls are your opponent's Combat points. The aim is to cross them all out, and you must do this within a certain number of rounds. One skull is one Combat point. The number of rounds you have to defeat your opponent is shown to the left beneath their name.

At the start of each round, you decide how strong an attack to launch against your opponent. You have two options:

Standard attack
Roll 7 or more: your opponent loses 1 Combat point

Power attack
Roll 9 or more: your opponent loses 3 Combat points

Once you've chosen, roll two dice. **Remember, if you choose to roll for '7 or more' but actually roll a 10, you still only score the points for '7 or more'.**

If you go for a Power attack, your chances of success are lower – but you only have a limited number of rounds in which to cross out all your opponent's Combat points. If you fail to do so, you must turn to the Defeat entry. Remember, defeat does not necessarily mean death.

Every time you fail to match your chosen roll, you must cross out one or more of your Life points. These are the hearts beneath your heading. One heart is one Life point. To find out how many to cross out, look at your opponent's Damage rating, which is shown to the right beneath their name. If your Life points are reduced to zero at any point in the combat, you are dead and your adventure is over.

Before the fight starts, check your Log Book to see how many Life points you have. Then turn back to the combat entry, and cross out any hearts needed to show the correct amount. Once the fight is over, update your Log Book if you lost any Life points.

If you're fighting more than one opponent, you must choose which opponent you want to attack before every roll. You don't have to defeat one opponent before moving on to the next, but you must defeat all your opponents before turning to the Victory entry.

For a step-by-step example of how combat works, turn to the back of the book.

PICTURE PUZZLES

There are ten picture puzzles, but which ones you encounter will depend on the choices you make on your journey. If you solve a puzzle correctly, it will reveal an entry number to turn to. If you can't solve the puzzle, you'll be given a different entry number. But don't give up too soon, or your quest could come to an unhappy end.

Read the text that leads into the puzzle closely – often there will be clues there to help you. And remember that you won't always be able to solve the puzzle simply by looking at the picture. Sometimes you'll have to move or bend the page to reveal the answer...

USBORNE QUICKLINKS

If you don't have two dice for the combat, you can use an online dice roller instead. For links to an online dice roller, and also to print out extra copies of the Log Book, go to usborne.com/Quicklinks and enter 'Curse Breaker', or simply scan the QR code below.

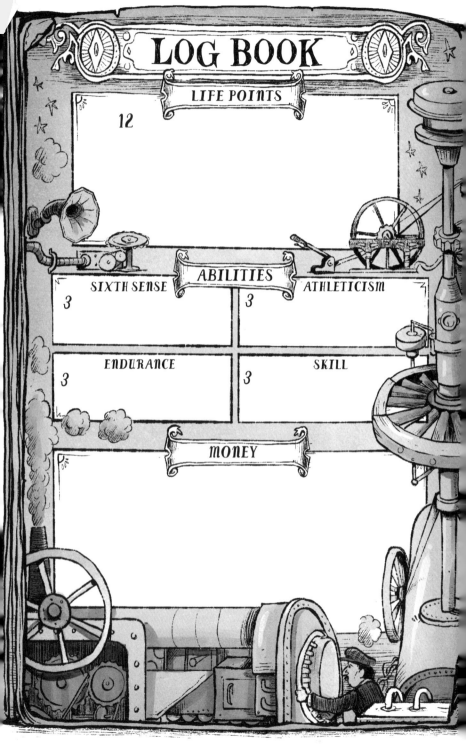

LOG BOOK

LIFE POINTS

12

ABILITIES

SIXTH SENSE

3

ATHLETICISM

3

ENDURANCE

3

SKILL

3

MONEY

ITEMS

NOTES

I

Far below, the nightwatchman calls the hour from the citadel wall. Your chain clinks as you shuffle across to the window – just a small cross cut into the tower. The cold air makes your sleepless eyes water. Outside, the lamplit streets fade into the ancient city of Mirewick, and your eyes are drawn to the horizon. Soon it will be dawn. The cell door will open and you'll be taken down to the Field of Healing to be executed. You know the way well. You've led many prisoners along the same path as a guard. The executioner will be waiting, head respectfully bowed beneath a grey hood, and when you reach the block you'll be thanked for the sacrifice you're about to make for Mayor Eldritch and The Order.

Looking out at the bright stars, the question that turns over in your mind is 'Why?' It was just a single word whispered in your ear. You remember the prisoner leaning over. Her breath on your cheek.

"Skerramore."

So faint that no one else could hear. Skerramore. What could be so dangerous about that forgotten place that you have to die?

Suddenly you freeze. There's a sound outside your cell. Soft footsteps that stop, and a key turning in the lock. The door inches open and something lands in the straw by your feet. You grab it as the footsteps fade. It's a key. Unfastening your chain, you creep forwards. The corridor is empty. To your right is a door that opens onto the hollow centre of the tower. The way out lies this way. To your left are more cells, and from this direction you hear the muffled cries of an inmate. It sounds like the man they brought in last night, yelling something you couldn't quite catch.

If you'd like to go right, turn to **305**.

If you'd like to go left, turn to **244**.

2

Do you have the FORTUNE TELLER'S CARDS?

If so, turn to **295**.

If not, turn to **199**.

3

It's an old woman with a yellow bonnet. She stops and turns.

"Seagrave?"

It's Ada!

"Come on," she cries. "No time for gawking!"

Suddenly there are people rushing past you, a small band, following Ada down to the steps.

"Don't give them time to get in your head!" she cries, lobbing a firecracker at the men in top hats.

Her gang attacks with desperate speed – hacking and slashing and driving them down the steps and into the arms of the frenzied sleepwalkers. But the top hats fight back, drawing night-sabres from their long canes and forming a tight ring on the riverbank. The monster hangs over them all, dripping water in the moonlight.

If you have the SMOKE BOMB and would like to use it, turn to **345**.

If you have the SLEEPING POTION and would like to use it, turn to **246**.

If you have neither, or don't want to use them, turn to **188**.

4

If you have 2 SHILLINGS, turn to **224**.

If not, turn to **367**.

5

The crowd gasps, and Orson looks at you for a moment in disbelief.

"We should put you on display," he says. "Come and see the world's unluckiest human. Quick, before the cage is hit by lightning."

He leans in and whispers roughly in your ear.

"Don't ask to play again – you'll scare off all my customers."

The crowd parts as you step down from the stage, as if your bad luck could be catching.

Turn to **53**.

6

The last guard slumps against the railings. He reaches for his key, as if he could somehow escape through the gates. Gently, you ease it from his grasp. He sighs and falls still. Glancing over your shoulder, you open the gates and slip through.

Turn to **76**.

7

You feel your body crumple, your eyes closing, and the last thing you see is the Watcher, silent and still. But her lips... did they... did they move? Then only darkness.

No, not only that. Because suddenly you hear a polite cough, and a voice saying, "Welcome to The Last Gasp Hotel. We hope you have a pleasant stay."

Slowly, you open one eye. You're in an elevator, and the attendant smiles and slides open a decorative metal gate. But there's something about him... Something strange... And then you see why he's smiling. Why he's *always* smiling. It's because he's a ventriloquist's dummy. His arm reaches out jerkily to direct you into a long corridor filled with doors. The gate closes behind you, and the lift goes up. You pull the bell chain to call it back, but it doesn't return.

"It won't work, Seagrave."

It's Eldritch. You can't see her, but her voice echoes down the corridor.

"Things like that never do in dreams. But of course – silly of me! You wouldn't know that, would you?"

You try one of the doors. It's locked. You try another. She laughs, and this time the laughter rises higher and higher until it's something inhuman. You clamp your hands over your ears.

If you want to ask her to open one of the doors, turn to **262**.

If you want to ask who she is, turn to **333**.

8

The man laughs and bows theatrically as you pass.

"I'm much obliged, officer. Much obliged."

Delete all the SHILLINGS from your LOG BOOK, then turn to **162**.

Add your SKILL and SIXTH SENSE levels.

If your total is 9 or higher, turn to **286**.

If it's 8 or lower, turn to **202**.

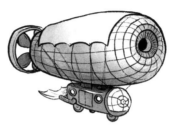

10

The guard puts a shaky finger to his lips, and you nod. In the moonlight you see the people's blank stares, their glassy eyes. And then you hear a strange noise, hollow yet high-pitched, as if from a great sea-creature. The effect on them is immediate. As one they turn and shuffle off in the direction of the noise. The guard waits until the last one's gone, then stands up. You ask what's going on.

"What do you mean?" he says. "They're sleepwalkers, aren't they?"

You wait for him to say more, but he clearly thinks no further explanation is necessary.

"How did you get so wet?" he asks.

Your hand goes to your wet clothes, but he turns and walks away without waiting for an answer. You stare at the empty square, and the dragon's words echo in your head: '*First people lose their dreams, then they lose their minds*'.

If you decide to follow him into the city, turn to **174**.

If you want to see where all the sleepwalkers went, turn to **45**.

11

Your fingers brush the back railing as your desperate dive falls just short. You look up to see the rear carriage disappearing down the line. Meg pokes her head out from your coat and chatters angrily. Slowly, painfully, you get to your feet and begin the climb back up the hill. You have no idea how long it will be until the next train, and you're tired of waiting. You decide to go by airship.

Turn to **34**.

12

The cries of the showmen rise above the music and crowds. A man with a shiny red waistcoat throws his arm in the air and bellows:

"Step right this way, ladies and gents! Take the hammer, sir, and show the lady your true worth. Or why not you, miss? Show that strength can reside in a form so fair!"

Further on, children are gathered around the 'Whac-a-troll'. You watch the little green troll popping its head out of hole after hole, chattering angrily each time the mallet comes down.

Suddenly, a man leans down and looks you in the eye.

"Care to try your luck?"

He's standing under a sign with 'Orson's Wheel of Fortune' written in gold lettering. Next to him is a spinning wheel divided into equal segments numbered from one to six.

"A shilling a play. Just spin the wheel and if it lands on a four, five or six, you get two back. I can't say fairer than that."

He spreads his arms wide and does a little half-bow, revealing a bald patch behind his carefully combed fringe.

If you'd like to play, turn to **300**.

If you decide to walk on past, turn to **53**.

13

Slowly, reluctantly, you walk back up the lane. She wipes her eyes with the back of her hand, smearing the black and white paint.

"What do you want?" she asks in a small, tired voice. "You won, didn't you?"

You point out that she's taken one of your items. You say it as much to cheer her up as to ask for it back. She seems a different person.

"Take it, take it," she says, handing it back. "I don't know why I took it."

You ask what she means, but don't get a response. She lies on the floor and stares blankly down the lane.

"Sleep," she mutters softly. "I want sleep."

You can't stay here any longer. Carefully, you move her into a doorway and leave the lane.

Add the returned item to your LOG BOOK, then turn to **335**.

14

Gently lifting the cloak, you see a small dog curled up underneath. It whines softly as the rain wets its fur, but it doesn't wake. With your heart hammering you take the cloak and fall back into the crowd.

Add the CLOAK to your LOG BOOK, then turn to **198**.

15

Your final bolt enters the monster's mouth just as it's about to shoot. There's a choking, gargling sound, and then silence. The long neck hangs limp, its white fur bloodied, and swinging from the end is the strange, troll-like head.

Pulling down your sleeve, you carry on through the ravine. There's a steep scramble beside a chuckling stream, and then your path slips back into the quiet forest.

Gain 1 ABILITY point, then turn to **356**.

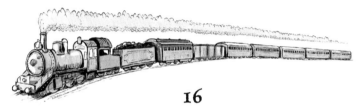

16

You run back along the walkway and there's a sudden rushing sound as the water gets sucked down and explodes upwards. Water and ice rain down, and you're too slow to avoid a chunk of ice striking you painfully between the shoulder blades.

Deduct 1 LIFE point, then turn to **216**.

17

As you follow the road through the outskirts of Mirewick, it starts to rain. Mill workers join you from the rows of red-brick houses on either side. They're on their way in for the morning shift, heads down, boots tramping over the wet cobbles. Soon, they've formed a thick, slow-moving crowd in front of you. You're torn between wanting to get off the streets as quickly as possible, and not wanting to draw attention to yourself.

If you decide to force your way through, turn to **149**.

If you decide to walk at the pace of the crowd, turn to **97**.

18

You run across and the men in top hats turn. The guard straightens up, gasping.

"I let a sleepwalker escape," he says. "I was trying to help her."

One of the men looks at you with cold, grey eyes. You remember what you saw in the mirror – the hollow socket, the metal teeth. Why can't you see them without the mirror?

"There's nothing you can do," he says to the guard.

"She will never sleep again," the other says.

"And The Order will be maintained."

You look from one to the other and ask why she can't sleep.

"Because she is missing something. You all are."

"But none of you know it."

"Not even you, Seagrave."

The two men draw their lips back and make a strange rasping sound. You realise they're laughing, and it hones your anger to a cold, hard point. You tell them you know more than they realise. You know about the dreams. You know they're not human.

"And there's something you're missing, too," you say. "Something you haven't been able to lay your claws on all this time."

"And what's that, Seagrave?" they ask in unison.

"Me."

They hiss as your hand flies to your sabre.

Rounds: 5 Damage: 2

YOU

If you win, turn to **307**.

If you lose, turn to **139**.

19

"What's your name?" the woman calls, as the light fades from the porthole.

"Seagrave," you shout, above the noise of the engine.

"Seagrave," she repeats. "I'm Ada."

"Where are we going?"

"This canal will take us out below Pendle Rise," she shouts, before tying a shawl over her mouth to block the fumes.

You shut the cabin door and sit down on the bed. You think of the city slipping by above your head, and for the first time in weeks, you start to relax. Grabbing a cushion, you lie back to rest your eyes...

"SEAGRAVE!"

The shout tips you from the bed onto the cabin floor.

"Get out here!"

You scramble outside and for a moment it feels like you're still dreaming. The boat is floating through the rooftops, high above the city streets. The cold wind whistles through your hair, and you grip the cabin door to steady yourself. You're on the old aqueduct.

"Look!" Ada shouts, pointing behind.

A train is gaining on you fast, running on a viaduct built alongside. She hands you a telescope. One of the wagons is open at the side and filled with guards, and... what's that? You look closer and see something metallic, with cogs and a winding mechanism.

"They've got a ballista!" you yell. "They're going to shoot us from the sky!"

"A ballista?" Ada cries.

"A giant crossbow!"

"Not if we get them first!" she shouts. "Look in the hold, under the canvas. There's a panel that slides open. I'll anchor us in place to give you a clear shot. And Seagrave," she grabs your arm as you duck through the door. "You might only get one."

You rush through and find a ballista mounted on the deck. Sliding the panel aside, you hear the engine slow and feel the anchor hold. Now is your shot. As the wind whistles past, you swing the bow around and stare out at the train. To hit it, you need to know exactly how fast it's travelling.

Turn the page, and when you think you know the train's speed, go to that entry number.

If you can't work it out, turn to **190**.

9

BOLTS

WIND SPEED

OIL LEVEL

You stumble backwards up the stairs, slashing, kicking, doing whatever you can to keep the beast's jaws from your throat. You fall into the courtyard and slam the doors shut. They shudder under the impact from within, but hold firm. Deduct 1 ABILITY point.

After catching your breath, you weigh your options. There are two routes to the Citadel that seem best. And remember that now you're above ground again, you need to roll two DICE at the end of each entry, following the same instructions as before.

If you'd like to go past the cotton mill, turn to **274**.

If you'd like to cut through the backstreets where the mill workers live, turn to **110**.

21

Madame Esther finds the card and lays it next to the other two. She mutters some words under her breath, and the scene in the room starts to shift. The sunlight fades and the hands of the clock spin around and around. A door opens from behind and light from the landing falls across the floorboards. There's a shadow, and like in a dream, you already know who it is. Your dad, who's been dead ten years. In silence, he walks across to the blackboard and picks up the chalk. Only when he's finished does he turn around, looking at you expectantly, like when he was teaching you to read and write. But on the board is a single word. 'INVASION.' And he's drawn something. An umbrella and a top hat.

You reach out and gasp as your hand strikes the glass. You'd forgotten the ball, the fortune teller, everything but the room and your dad. But he's gone now. The ball is empty and lifeless once more. Gain 1 ABILITY point.

Madame Esther looks at you, and fear is etched across her face.

"Someone was trying to reach you. Someone more powerful than me."

You ask if she means your father, and she shakes her head.

"The vision was pieced together from your memories, that's why you saw your father. But the message is from someone else."

She looks at you across the table.

"What did it mean?"

You shake your head.

"I don't know."

She gathers up the three cards and hands them to you.

"Keep these. Maybe whoever reached you will try again."

You thank her and stash them safely away.

"Now go. The coast is clear, even if your future is not."

Add FORTUNE TELLER'S CARDS to your LOG BOOK, then turn to **303**.

22

You follow a small trail that runs above a black river fringed with ice. The roots of an old tree grow across the path, and as you step between them, your foot plunges through the snow into thin air. Roots and dead leaves flash past as you tumble into the mouth of a cave. Hitting the ground hard, you look up. Two long fangs shift in the dim light. They curve over a brown muzzle that's getting a light dusting of snow. The muzzle parts and lets out a low growl. You've disturbed the hibernation of a sabre-toothed grizzly bear!

If you've got SLEEPING POTION, turn to **89**.

If not, turn to **292**.

23

You snap to the side and feel the rush of air past your cheek. His fist connects with the face of someone who was coming up behind. The unlucky man is out cold before he hits the floor. His companions look at him in shock for a moment, then turn to the culprit. You take advantage of the distraction and slip away without saying a word.

Gain 1 ABILITY point, then turn to **198**.

24

You take your meal onto the street. The gravy is thick and hot, and the tea is strong. You let Meg steal a bite, and wipe your chin as you feel some of your strength returning.

Add 6 LIFE points, deduct 1 SHILLING from your LOG BOOK, then turn to **177**.

25

Your aim is true. The bottle smashes on the bricks beside the fisher's head, and the creature drops the cat and scurries further up the wall with an angry screech. The cat lands on its feet and disappears down the alley. Brushing a shard of glass from your shoulder, you turn back onto the lane.

Gain 1 ABILITY point, then turn to **334**.

26

You jump in the direction of travel and land smoothly.

Turn to **77**.

27

Your eye travels from the window to the gargoyle. From the gargoyle to the statue. There's something... are they pointing? Pointing to a painting on the wall? You walk up the stairs and look closely. There's a young woman on a swing hanging from a tree. She's all alone in a forest, her blue dress catching the sunlight, and you hear birdsong. It takes a moment to register. Birdsong? She looks at you and smiles as the dress ripples and the swing completes its arc.

"Hello," she says. "What year is it?"

You stammer a reply, and she muses for a moment as she swings. "Two hundred and twenty years," she says, almost to herself.

The ropes creak against the bough.

"The forest does strange things to time, you know."

She looks at you closely.

"I don't like the latest fashion."

"It's a guard's uniform," you explain, smoothing it down self-consciously.

"A guard?" she cries, stopping and glaring mid-swing. "I didn't call a guard!"

You quickly explain about Malory and she relaxes.

"Poor Malory," she murmurs. "But an unknown in Skerramore..."

She looks down at her bare stockinged feet.

"Still, I suppose the house likes you. What's your name?"

You reply, and she reaches into the folds of her dress and takes something out. A looking glass, except the glass is missing, it's only the frame.

"Take this then, Seagrave."

She walks towards you and reaches out. The frame emerges from the painting, a skeleton hand gripping the handle. You take it and the hand withdraws.

"Who are you?" you ask.

"Mary Finch, 27th Watcher of Skerramore."

You nod and breathe deeply. You feel faint. The looking glass seems to swell in your vision, and the stairs slip away beneath you.

Gain 1 ABILITY point and add the LOOKING GLASS to your LOG BOOK. Then roll one DICE and add your ENDURANCE level.

If your total is 8 or higher, turn to **141**.

If it's 7 or lower, turn to **319**.

28

The wheel comes to a stop and Orson gives a theatrical wince. "Ah, that's the way it goes. Do you fancy another spin, perhaps? A chance to get your money back?"

He scratches his chin, as if thinking.

"No, maybe that's not enticing enough. Let's double the stake, and I'll pay double too. That way you'd come out ahead. And I tell you what else I'll do, because I don't like to see an honest guard out of pocket, I'll shorten your odds. All you have to do is spin a three or above."

He puffs out his cheeks and shakes his head, as if he can't quite believe what he's saying. The crowd murmurs its approval.

If you'd like to have another go, turn to **277**.

If not, turn to **53**.

29

She looks out over the water.

"I can't get anyone to listen. The guards, the politicians. They say they don't believe me. Pretend I'm mad. But... I don't know. I think they *do* believe me. So what does that mean?"

She meets your eye.

"Listen, Seagrave. I think the guards are the least of our worries. It's not them that's attacking the sleepwalkers. It's not them that controls that thing."

"It's the men in top hats," you say.

She nods.

If you want to ask another question, turn to **308**.

If you want to get on your way, turn to **365**.

30

A terrifying shriek tears you from your stupor. The old woman's face is inches from your own, but it's no longer human. The eyes are white and blind and the teeth are too large for her jaws. They glint in the firelight, long and rusted. Made of iron. She stumbles back clutching her hand, and her nails are long and claw-like.

"What is that?" she cries. "Around your neck."

You clasp the pendant and feel it pulsing under your palm. She wrings her hands and seems to shrivel before your eyes. Her cries are strange and unearthly. You turn away, and when you turn back, there's nothing left but a white dress and the metal teeth.

Make a note of the number of this entry (30).

Then, if this is the first time the pendant's been used, turn to **155**.

If it's the second time, turn to **314**.

Then, turn to **42**.

3I

You uncork the bottle and drop it to the ground, letting the yellow gas seep out. You move to the edge of the crowd and watch nervously as the town guards start to make their way through, checking the faces of each prisoner they pass.

"Vile creature, you shall pay for this infamy!"

Up on stage, Edmund is reaching a crescendo, one hand raised to the heavens, the other resting bravely on the hilt of his sabre. He fixes his opponent with a look of righteous rage, but his composure is disturbed by a peal of laughter from the crowd. His mouth twitches, but he ploughs on.

"Defend yourself, sir! And feel the keen edge of my revenge!"

A loud belly-laugh shakes the man's resolve, and he turns to face the crowd.

"Peace, good people! This is a most tragical moment in our performance."

"Good people?" someone shouts. "Has he forgotten where he is?!"

"I know it very well. And it would be wise to listen well. Let our tears bring forth the green shoots of change!"

He strikes a heroic pose, hand clenched to his chest, waiting for the applause. There's a moment's silence, and then the crowd roars with laughter. The prison guards try to calm things down, but they're struggling to keep a straight face, too. A boot sails through the air in a perfect arc and strikes Edmund on the nose. You can just about hear him above the noise.

"You dare, sir? You dare?"

He launches himself into the crowd and more actors follow, running out from behind the stage. Cries of delight mix with the laughter as the prisoners surge to meet them. The town guards are swept forwards in the melee, shouting and holding on to their hats. Your plan couldn't have worked any better. In the confusion you slip away and run the short distance to the woods.

Gain 1 ABILITY point, then turn to **44**.

32

You move left to cramp the guard's strike. His sabre scrapes the wall, slowing it just enough for you to grab his arm and twist it around hard. The weapon drops from his grasp and a blow to the back of the neck drops the guard too. You look up. The corridor's empty. A prisoner cries out from a nearby cell, but there's nothing you can do for her. You whip off the guard's sabre-belt and thread it around your waist, then rush back towards the hollow tower.

Add the NIGHT-SABRE to your LOG BOOK, then turn to **305**.

33

You step through into the carriage beyond. A corridor runs along the right-hand side, with doors opening onto small compartments, and you make your way down until you find one that's empty. Settling by the window, you see a suitcase on the rack above and a newspaper on the seat by the door. It looks like the compartment isn't empty after all. You lean over and read the headline: '*Eldritch Calms Fears in Sleepwalker Mystery*'. You imagine her jabbing a sleepwalker with her umbrella and smile. She doesn't seem the sort to scare easily.

A few minutes later, a man walks in with a black top hat perched above his hard, pinched face. The Watcher's words echo through your mind, but you suppress the urge to get up. You know lots of people that wear top hats, and besides, where would you go as the train clatters along the tracks?

Instead, you turn to watch the outskirts of the city pass by. The carriage is warm and the sun low in the sky. A steward wheels down a trolley serving tea and biscuits, and you break off a few crumbs for Meg inside your coat. You've hardly slept for days, and Mount Scarfell is many hours away. With a last glance at the man in the corner, you fall into a deep sleep.

Add 5 LIFE points and turn to **315**.

34

The aerodrome is nearby, on the outskirts of Mirewick.

"How are you with heights, Meg?"

You're walking down the hill, and as if in reply, she hooks her tail onto an overhanging branch and swings from tree to tree. Below, you see the airships tethered to their mooring masts – some big enough to transport a hundred people, some much smaller. The smaller ones are what you're after. Flown by a single aeronaut who negotiates their own rates. But finding one willing to fly you to the Whistling Mountains won't be easy.

You spot a red airship at the edge of the airfield, and even from here you can see strips of yellow and blue where it's been patched up with whatever material was to hand. You smile to yourself and hurry downhill.

Avoiding the main terminal, you clamber over the low fence and make your way across the grass. Above you, the red airship sways gently in the breeze, its nose tethered to the mast. The words of an old sea shanty drift down, and you start climbing the steps. The singer is at the top, swabbing the gangplank. You introduce yourself and he cups an ear.

"What was that? *Seagrave!*" He slams his mop into the bucket and roars with laughter. "There's a pretty name to take on a voyage!"

He turns his back and carries on with his cleaning.

"Where do you want to go?"

You tell him and the mop stops.

"Interesting."

"Can you do it?"

He turns around and looks you up and down with a shrewd eye. Eventually he scratches his grey beard.

"You hand over your sabre till we land and I won't ask why you're avoiding those guards over there in the terminal." He jerks a thumb over his shoulder. "Agreed?"

You nod.

"Now there's not many here who could get you to the Whistling Mountains in one piece. And none who'd take a known fugitive."

He spits over the gangplank.

"What I'm saying is, I don't come cheap."

You show him the card the butler gave you and he grins.

"That'll do. Captain Gambrel, at your service."

Turn to **265**.

35

The smoke from the funnel – it's going straight up. The train must be moving the same speed and direction as the wind! You adjust your aim and release the trigger. The whole boat rocks as the ballista fires. You jump aside to avoid the recoil, so Ada is the first to see.

"A hit! A direct hit!"

Gain 1 ABILITY point, then turn to **366**.

36

The circle has closed, silent and menacing. There's nothing you can say that won't sound like a lie. Nothing except the truth. And so you tell them about your escape from the Citadel, your flight across the city.

"I found someone who told me to come here. She said there was something I needed to see."

In the silence that follows you hear the blood pounding through your ears. If they don't like what you've said, there's no escape. The old imp turns her painted eyes to the mountaintop hidden by the trees, as if seeking guidance.

"Then go," she says at last. "And disturb us no more. We lived in Mirewick once. Chimney sweeps, sewer cleaners, that was us. But we left long ago and did not wish to be found."

The circle parts to let you pass, but you pause and turn back.

"Your eyes..." you begin.

"Are closed to all the dreamless ones. Perhaps it keeps out the lie."

You ask what she means, and she points over the horizon towards Mirewick.

"What you see there is not the truth. There is a lie rotting its heart."

Her arm drops.

"Something is stealing your dreams."

You open your mouth, but she turns towards the mountain.

"Go. Perhaps you will find your answers up there."

Turn to **129**.

37

Skirting the edge of the clearing, you press on through the trees. Strangely, the snowstorm dies down almost as quickly as it started, and you start to warm up.

Turn to **356**.

38

You look up and see the stars are starting to fade. Dawn is approaching. As you make your way through the streets you catch glimpses of the Citadel, its lamps glowing faintly on the hill. What will you do when you get there? You've had no time to stop and think. In the silence of a small courtyard, you take the mirror from your coat pocket. It feels light in your hands, and the glass is smooth now. No sign of the cracks that showed Eldritch's face. Although... there is a slight smudge there... you rub it with your sleeve, but the smudge remains. No, it's moving. You lean closer and almost drop the mirror. It's not a smudge, it's a slow stream of ghostly figures, flowing through the reflected sky like a pale river! But before you can take a closer look, a voice behind your back makes you jump.

"How interesting. Do you mind if I take a look?"

A tall, thin figure in a top hat looms over the glass. And this time you do drop the mirror. Your cry sounds loud in the courtyard and you spin around. The man's face is the same as before, pale and drawn. But the glass showed something different. Something monstrous.

"I think I'd better have that."

He leans down to grasp the mirror with his long, white fingers, and you see that hideous face reflected again in the glass. Is this what they really are, these men in top hats? Are they not even human? His voice is soft and dangerous.

"Where were you going with it, I wonder..."

You feel a strange sensation inside your head that makes you shudder. A probing and prodding as memories flash unbidden through your mind. He's searching for the answer you won't give him, and with a great effort, you draw your sabre.

If you have the PENDANT, turn to **344**.

If you never had it, or have deleted it, turn to **237**.

39

Leaving the square, you make your way towards the prison grounds. You know the general direction, but the Doldrums is a tangle of lanes, and you realise you've turned down a dead end. You hear a girlish laugh behind you.

"You don't know where you're going. Oh dear."

You spin around and see a young woman holding a thin cane casually over one shoulder. One side of her face is painted black and the other is painted white, and she's wearing a prison uniform.

"What mood am I in?" she wonders aloud. "Heads or tails?"

If you want to call 'heads', turn to **226**.

If you want to call 'tails', turn to **103**.

40

You look down at Meg, and she climbs up onto your shoulder. Slowly, you stand, and the butler nods.

"Very good. Please follow me."

He lights a lamp and leads you down a long, twisting flight of stairs. The air gets colder the deeper you go, until finally you enter a small cave. Inside is a door made of burnished gold.

"Beyond is the Other Side," he whispers. "It will shape itself to your wishes. The 27th chose a woodland. You may, of course, choose somewhere different."

You turn to Meg. You always wanted to go on a voyage. Just a small boat with a sail, and the horizon beyond. She chatters excitedly and leaps from you to the butler, then back to you.

He takes off his glasses and pretends to clean them, hiding a tear.

"It sounds like you're ready for another adventure, Seagrave."

You turn to the door and see your face reflected, calm and glowing.

"I think I am."

41

White ridges pass beneath you like ghostly waves. It's so dark you hardly see them until another flash shows just how close they are. Thunder rolls as your ship ploughs on.

Roll one DICE.

If you roll an even number, turn to **130**.

If you roll an odd number, turn to **354**.

42

Your breath comes in short, sharp gasps. What was that? Meg cautiously sniffs the steaming clothes and then climbs back into your coat. The smell of brimstone fills the cottage, and as you close the door, you take deep gulps of cold, fresh air before carrying on up the mountain.

Turn to **356**.

43

The square had grand origins. The lampposts are stamped with the shield of Mirewick, and there's an old fountain with a forgotten goddess pouring water from an urn. Now, half of her head is missing, and the water trickles down one arm, covering her side in green algae. But not far from where she stands, there's a new statue of pure white marble. It shows an elegant lady in a tall top hat – Mayor Eldritch. Leader for the last twenty years and architect of The Order. Her hands rest on the handle of her umbrella and her head is tilted to the sky. On the plinth are the words: "Together, we dream a better world".

Beyond the statue is a marketplace filled with ragtag stalls. It's quiet at this early hour, with the rain steadily falling, and you make your way across to have a look around. Outside one stall, a grizzled old man sits on a canvas chair. He doesn't look up from his book, but rests a hand on the head of a large dog. It growls quietly as you pass.

"Over here, officer," calls a woman with long black hair. "There's a cure for every sickness." In her stall, jars glint in the candlelight.

In the end, you find nine items that might be of use:

MINIATURE CROSSBOW with 12 BOLTS – 3 SHILLINGS

Straps to your wrist. Bolts propelled by an explosive charge for extra power. Remember to make a note of the number of bolts.

GRAPPLING HOOK – 2 SHILLINGS

Rope with a hook that helps you climb.

SMOKE BOMB – 2 SHILLINGS

Releases a cloud of thick smoke to hide your movements.

SAFE CRACKER – 2 SHILLINGS

A drill and explosive charge, used to blow the door off a small safe.

LAUGHING VAPOUR – 2 SHILLINGS

Renders people (but not creatures) helpless with laughter.

SLEEPING POTION – 2 SHILLINGS

Sends a person or creature to sleep.

HERBAL TONIC – 1 SHILLING

Drink that restores 2 LIFE points. Make a note that you can only use this **after** completing an entry, but **before** turning to the next one. Once used, delete it from your LOG BOOK.

ENERGY POTION – 1 SHILLING

Gives you a sudden energy boost. If you buy this, make a note that it adds 1 to your dice roll. So if you roll 8, the potion makes it 9. The effect lasts for one fight. After your chosen fight, you must delete it from your LOG BOOK.

CLOAK – 2 SHILLINGS

Keeps you warm and hides your uniform.

You're unsure how much of your limited funds to spend, but add any items you buy to your LOG BOOK along with their notes, and deduct the correct number of SHILLINGS. You can only buy **one of any item**, and remember you can only use these items when given the option in the text (except for the herbal tonic or energy potion).

Turn to **228**.

44

You follow a trail deeper into the woods. Small headstones poke through the undergrowth, pale in the dark green light. A rusty harmonica lies by one, and above you a crow caws. You hurry on.

Finally the trees thin out, and you see the fence, and a gate. Marching up with a confident stride, you greet the guard. He has no reason to suspect anything, and you don't give him one. He nods his head and swings the gate wide. You join a towpath running alongside one of Mirewick's many canals, and on the other side a hill rises behind a crumbling brick wall. You've reached Pendle Rise at last.

Turn to **221**.

45

The sleepwalkers move in a silent mass down to the river. The moonlight shimmers on the dark, slow water, and little waves appear on the surface. You watch from the embankment as the waves grow larger, choppier, and the river swells as a great, eel-like monster bursts forth! Its head is a giant, circular mouth, with small, hooked teeth spiralling down its throat. The sleepwalkers cry out, and it's the sound of people who no longer know what's real and what's nightmare. They scramble for the steps back up to the embankment, and that's when you notice the men in top hats. They stride in from the streets and raise a dull, hollow chant. "The Order will be maintained. The Order will be maintained."

You feel someone brush past.

If you have (or had) the PENDANT, turn to **3**.

If not, turn to **193**.

46

While you flounder behind, her feet hardly leave prints. Finally, sinking up to your knees in a deep drift, you fall on your back. Your breath rises through the branches, and you realise you'll never catch her. At least it won't be hard to retrace your steps.

Turn to **129**.

47

If you want to try stealing a pie, turn to **115**.

If you decide to leave the shop, turn to **177**.

48

You steady yourself and leap. Pieces of the great hall spin past as the groan turns to a scream so loud that the vortex shimmers and breaks apart in your vision until only Eldritch and the Watcher remain, her hands outstretched. The moment before you touch, she smiles – and then there's a flash. Add 1 ABILITY point.

Turn to **389**.

49

She sighs and accepts your item with bad grace.

"Spoilsport! I just wanted to play a little."

As you leave the lane, you risk a look over your shoulder. She's standing where you left her, tears running down her face. You hesitate.

If you want to go back and ask why she's crying, turn to **13**.

If you decide to continue on your way, turn to **335**.

50

Your footsteps echo as you make your way down, and the door opens onto a spiral staircase – the way you came in!

Gain 1 ABILITY point, then turn to **326**.

51

A man in a top hat seems to appear out of nowhere.

"The Order will be maintained," he hisses, lunging towards you.

MAN IN TOP HAT

Rounds: 5   Damage: 2

YOU

If you win, turn back to the **previous entry** to continue on your way.

If you lose, turn to **80**.

52

You tell her you won't pay a penny more than two shillings.

Roll one DICE and add your SIXTH SENSE level.

If your total is 6 or higher, turn to **350**.

If it's 5 or lower, turn to **176**.

53

Leaving the Wheel of Fortune behind, you make your way past the House of Mirrors, the House of Horrors and the Laughing Clown. You turn to look at him, sitting on a pedestal high above the crowds. His hands grip the armrests, knuckles white, and his laughter doesn't stop or waver as tears stream down his painted face.

Further along, you notice a disturbance in the crowds up ahead. Guards! They're making enquiries, and someone points in your direction. You slip down a passageway between two tents and hurry away from the main thoroughfare. Did they see you? Frantically, you look for somewhere to duck out of sight on this long canvas aisle. And then you notice a gap, and the black and purple drapes of the fortune teller's stall. Madame Esther – Mistress of the Unknown. It looks so out of place, tucked away where no one will see it. You lift the drapes and walk through.

Incense swirls in the gloom. Esther sits facing you, long, red hair framing a heart-shaped face. She's young, which you weren't expecting, but the candlelight makes black wells of her eyes.

"Sit down," she murmurs.

Still standing, you ask why her stall is in such an odd spot.

"I'd say it was exactly where it was needed, wouldn't you?" she replies, picking up a deck of cards.

You look at her for a moment, before walking across to the table. A cloth is draped over a crystal ball, and as you sit down, it starts to glow, soft and pale. Esther's hands stop mid-shuffle.

"Is that your doing?" she asks, and you shake your head.

Slowly, tentatively, she lifts away the cloth. The ball flares, like a gas lamp being lit.

"It wants to show you something," she whispers.

She places the top two cards face up on the table.

"Find the third card to reveal the message. You must choose. The ball will guide you."

Leaning forward, you peer into the glass. At first, all you see is mist. Then it clears and you're in your childhood room, back how it was, with your toys spread out and sunlight slanting through the window. It's strange, but that's how you always remember it, warm and bright and... safe. Yes. That's it. Where did that feeling go? Even the weather seems different now.

Turn the page to see your old room. There are clues in there to a number. When you think you've found it, the fortune teller will place the card with that number next to the other two cards on her table. Add up all three numbers, then turn to that entry.

If you can't find the number, turn to **120**.

54

The dragon bows its head slightly in acknowledgement.

Add 1 ABILITY point, then turn to **159**.

55

There's only so long you can wave the looking glass around before you start feeling foolish, and that moment passed a while ago. Deduct 1 ABILITY point.

Suddenly Meg chatters excitedly. She runs along your arm and pulls on your hand to line the frame up with the icy lake above. She jabs a tiny finger at the glass and you look closer. The lines and shadows on the ice join with the cracks on the glass to form a picture, a face.

"Eldritch," you whisper.

Turn to **211**.

* Hold the page with the mirror up to the light to see what Seagrave has just seen.

56

Her cane is a white blur, dancing, flying, biting, retreating, always just out of reach. You cry out as your night-sabre is sent spinning from your grasp. Evie flicks it up with her cane and catches it deftly by the handle. She laughs and presses the tip lightly against your throat. You fight the urge to swallow.

"Oh dear," she says. "Game's over."

You close your eyes and wait, but nothing happens. Cautiously, you open one eye. She looks confused.

"Game's over," she repeats. But her voice sounds different. Flat and weary.

Your night-sabre falls from her grasp. She passes a hand over her eyes and turns away.

"Where am I?" she mutters softly. "I'm so tired..."

You pick up your weapon and watch her walk down the lane, almost stumbling as she turns the corner.

Turn to **335**.

57

You haven't a moment to lose. You know there'll be more of those men in top hats here, but it's too crowded for the mirror. So trusting to luck and your own judgement, you weave your way through. On the stage you see the Watcher down on her knees. How did Eldritch find her? How is she even here? Your head spins as you remember the skeletal hand that passed you the mirror. But there she is with her head on the block. And suddenly you're at the front of the crowd with only a line of guards between you and Eldritch. You take out the mirror and angle it towards her.

"Look!" you shout. "Look what she is!"

Someone close to you laughs.

"Why don't you look yourself?" they call.

And you do. She looks the same, there in the glass. No hollow eye, no sabre-claws. Just an amused and victorious smile on her face.

"Hello, Seagrave. So nice of you to join us."

Two guards grab you and drag you onto the stage.

Turn to **171**.

58

You're about to slide open the hatch when the hairs on your neck stand up. You shrink back into the shadows. Bootsteps make themselves heard above the steady drip-drip of a leaking pipe. A guard walks past, night-sabre hanging from his hip. The inmate cries out and your muscles tense, but the guard doesn't stop. You hear the inmate pacing up and down his cell and creep to the door.

"Listen," you whisper. "Keep quiet."

He rushes across to the hatch and you inch it open. His eyes are bloodshot, one just a slit behind a swollen purple bruise. He stares at you intently as you ask him why he's there.

"Because they won't believe me," he hisses. "And it's almost too late."

"Too late?"

There's a pause.

"The invaders are coming."

You close your eyes. You've risked your life to talk to a madman. His eyes glaze over and he starts to whistle softly – a short, repetitive tune that lodges itself in your mind.

You turn to go.

Make a note of the prisoner's tune in your LOG BOOK. There may be a time in your adventure where you'll want to try whistling it. If there is, then immediately turn back fifty entries. If the new entry doesn't make sense, go back to the entry you were on.

If you'd like to explore the cells further, turn to **317**.

If you want to head back towards the hollow tower, turn to **305**.

59

You don't like the look of what you've just seen. There's a good chance every station in Mirewick is under watch by now. Not wanting to get any closer, you make a pretence of admiring the statue, then hurry back the way you came.

If you'd like to try train-hopping further down the line, turn to **182**.

Or if you'd like to charter an airship, turn to **34**.

60

You flip the second coin over and the girl catches it with the flicker of a smile. On the far side of the courtyard, a passageway leads deeper into the Doldrums. You're about to enter when you hear a shout. The girl runs across.

"Don't go down there," she says. "We call it Fisher Street."

She jerks her thumb at a doorway that looks like it's been boarded over for many years. Looking closer, you notice a small owl carved into the wood. She pulls, and the door swings open, boards and all. Steps lead down into darkness. You hesitate, until the girl lights a candle that was waiting at the bottom.

"Come on," she says impatiently, holding it up.

She leads you through a series of connecting cellars, rat droppings crunching underfoot. You have to duck to avoid hitting your head on the low beams.

"That owl," you say. "Did it mark a safe passage?"

Her shoulders stiffen and she doesn't reply. You remember your guard's uniform, and continue the rest of the way in silence. She leads you up another flight of stairs and pushes open the door at the top. It leads onto a large square.

"This is where you would've come out," she says, and before you can ask another question or even thank her, she shuts the door in your face. Another owl stares back.

Make a note of the owl symbol in your LOG BOOK. If you see another marked on a door at any point in your adventure, you can try opening the door by immediately turning back twenty entries.

Now, gain 1 ABILITY point, then turn to **43**.

61

You glance towards Blake. He's had more combat experience than you, and he points to where you should stand. It's no simple matter coordinating an attack like this. You spread out and advance. If Eldritch still has her staff, whenever you roll a double, you're hit by a lightning bolt, and must deduct 1 LIFE point regardless of whether you win or lose the round.

ELDRITCH

Rounds: 5   Damage: 3

YOU

If you win, turn to **185**.

If you lose, turn to **233**.

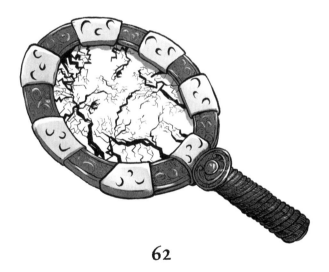

62

You gasp as the guard's sabre bites deep. Stumbling backwards, you're knocked to the ground and see the turmoil you've unleashed. Prisoners and guards are locked in battle, but their cries fade as you stare up at the grey sky and breathe your last.

63

In silence, she leads you through the Doldrums, twisting and turning and taking you further from Pendle Rise. You try to object, but she puts her finger to her lips and you think better of it. A steep passageway between two warehouses ends at a flaking green door with dark windows on either side.

"It's a lock-keeper's cottage," she says, bolting the door and lighting a lamp. "Or it was before the trains. They don't use the canal anymore, not this part... but I'm still here."

She chuckles and hangs up her wet shawl. Her back is bent, but her shoulders are broad. She stokes the fire and gestures for you to pull up an extra chair. Only when your coat and boots are steaming on the hearth does she sit down. You wait for her to start, but she seems lost in thought suddenly, staring into the flames. You notice her hands are raw and blackened by coaldust.

"Poor Silas. It was weeks without sleep. Months, even. Can you imagine what that does?"

You ask if she means the man in the paper, and she nods.

"But he's not the only one losing their mind. We call them sleepwalkers. There's more and more of them, and they can't remember a thing the next morning, but they've been up all night..."

She sighs.

"We keep track of strange happenings. That's what we do. The tune is our signal."

Suddenly she looks at you.

"Silas was probably hoping you were one of us..."

You look down. The fire crackles.

"Were you signalling to me?" you ask quietly.

"And why would I have done that?"

You tell her how a guard helped you escape the tower. And that the other prisoner whispered in your ear. Whispered 'Skerramore' – where you're heading now.

"I thought maybe they were part of your gang as well," you say.

But slowly she shakes her head.

"Skerramore on Pendle Rise... What's there but woodworm and ghosts?"

Her chin rests on her chest, her eyes deep in shadow.

Turn to **104**.

64

You nod slowly, and he grins and digs into your purse. His hand emerges with two coins, and he flips one up in the air, catching it deftly.

"Much obliged," he says.

With a mock bow he returns your purse and swaggers off to the tavern. There's a smattering of applause from the crowd, and you leave the scene without looking back.

Deduct 2 SHILLINGS, then turn to **162**.

65

Your eyes widen and your finger presses up against the glass.

"Look!" you say, pointing east. "Couldn't that inlet be a mouth? And that lake an eye? And just to the north – that's got to be the witch's nose!"

Gambrel looks over your shoulder and bursts out laughing.

"Never doubted you for a second, Seagrave! Not a second." He scratches his beard. "It never would have showed up on a map, neither."

Gain 1 ABILITY point, then turn to **270**.

66

In desperation you call out to the lady of the house.

"I nearly died getting here!" you cry, but there's no response. "They'll kill me!"

The butler discreetly clears his throat.

"I'm afraid you're wasting your time. My lady can't hear you."

You ask where she is.

"Somewhere neither you nor I can reach."

Defeated, you let him show you out. At the door he wishes you luck, but he can't meet your eye. Meg jumps onto his shoulder and watches you go. In the end, you make it beyond the borders of Mirewick before being spotted by a reconnaissance balloon on the northern moors. They hunt you down and transport your body back to the Citadel for identification.

67

You eye the guards closely. They're not going to let you through without good reason. Not into the grounds of a prison. And then the image of Evie Nightshade's strange, grinning face flashes through your mind. She's clearly escaped. They must be looking for her...

If you want to tell the guards you have information on Evie Nightshade, turn to **375**.

If you decide to follow the railings around and look for a point where you could climb over, turn to **98**.

68

Leaping for the grass verge, you clear the rails and roll down the slope. When you look up, the smoke from the train is already clearing. Meg pokes her head out to see what's happened.

"Change of plan," you say. "We'll go by air."

Turn to **34**.

69

You slip the cloak over your shoulders and pull the hood down low over your brow. Taking a deep breath, you walk past the gates and into the open road. The sirens wail in the distance. You move to the side, just enough to let them by, and your heart pounds as you draw near. But the question is still a shock when it comes.

"Who'd walk past four guards dressed like a thief in the night?" the leader wonders aloud.

Slowly, almost casually, he moves across your path. The others follow and you're forced to stop. He pulls back your hood and a grin spreads across his wolfish face.

"Well look who it is!"

You feel the icy edge of a night-sabre pressed against your side. You've been caught, and your execution will go ahead as planned.

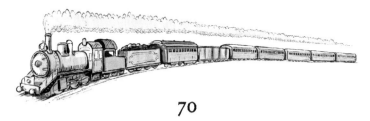

70

You turn off the cabin lamp but don't get any more sleep that night. The moon casts a pale, ghostly light over the marshes, showing glimpses of things you know can't be there, and it's a relief when the dawn light comes. You hear the squeak of the steward's trolley, and he serves you fried eggs and a round of toast, along with some steaming hot coffee. Add 3 LIFE points.

You ask him how long until the last stop, and he looks at you in surprise.

"Eight hours," he says. "But we only go there to turn round. There's nothing there."

He's right. It's mid-afternoon when you step off the train onto a deserted platform. Above you rises Demon's Well, or so you hope. It's flanked by pine forests and covered in fresh snow. Buttoning up your coat, you begin your climb. The locomotive almost sounds relieved as it toots its whistle and sets off back to Mirewick.

Turn to **137**.

71

Roll one DICE and add your ATHLETICISM level.

If your total is 8 or higher, turn to **355**.

If it's 7 or lower, turn to **132**.

72

Dawn is fast approaching. You put your head down and give the group a wide berth. It's the sensible move, and besides, you've no wish to attack someone you last saw selling stew in the market. You're nearly past when you hear a cry and see one of the guards staggering your way. He's struck in the back by the cook's shovel and collapses face-first on the cobbles. The giant cook lumbers over to retrieve his weapon, and behind him, the surviving guard turns tail and runs. That leaves you. The cook picks up his shovel. His bloodshot eyes narrow and you reluctantly draw your sabre.

SLEEPWALKER COOK

Rounds: 3   Damage: 2

YOU

If you win, turn to **253**.

If you lose, turn to **196**.

73

The last guard falls and you look up. The mill is filled with the twisted metal of broken machinery. Cotton dust hangs in the air and muffles the groans of the wounded. You run for the door, but have to grab hold of the frame to stop yourself falling through the hole where the staircase once stood. You spin around, looking for a way down. And then you see the beast by the window, bent over something on the ground. It stands up and wipes its mouth. Now's your chance! You run and jump.

Turn to **164**.

74

You parry blows that send a dull ache shooting up your arm. But your undoing almost comes from an unexpected quarter. The weight of the cook's attack sends one of the guards flying into you and knocks you to the ground. The sleepwalker lifts the shovel high above his head. Time seems to slow as you raise your arm, and then you see something small and dark streaking up his body. He bellows as Meg fastens herself to his face! She bites his finger as he tries to rip her off, and you tackle him to the ground. Before he can react, the hilt of your sabre connects with his head and the great body goes limp. Meg leaps onto your shoulder, and the remaining guard runs to his fallen companion. Kneeling down, he puts his ear to his chest. After a long moment, he closes the guard's eyes, and you bow your head.

"I know you, don't I?" he says. "You're Seagrave."

You stay silent, and he seems on the verge of saying something else, but then he gives a short laugh and looks back down at his friend.

"Good luck to you," he says softly.

You nod your thanks and look at the fallen bodies around you. Anger wells up inside, and as you turn towards the Citadel you swear vengeance against Mayor Eldritch and all her minions.

Turn to **122**.

75

Too late, you notice something being lifted above your head. Instinctively you try to grab it, and feel a biting pain as your fingers close over your own sabre! There's a chattering sound, and you see the tiny, grinning face of a fisher staring down.

"Thank you, Meg," the butler says calmly. "But your services won't be needed here."

The fisher makes a disappointed noise, drops the sabre at your feet and disappears inside the house.

Deduct 1 LIFE point, then turn to **294**.

An old castle stands on the brow of a hill, the flag of The Order flying from the turrets. That's where the inmates are kept. Its small, dark windows stare out across the park, and you turn aside to keep to the trees near the fence. A crow caws loudly, flying low towards the castle. You know a guard who works there, and you remember that one night, over a drink, he told you the prison felt more like an asylum these days. He'd shuddered while staring into the glowing embers of the stove. "The nights are worst," he said. "They can't sleep."

You hear loud voices up ahead and slow down. As the trees thin out, you see a crowd of prisoners gathered on the open grass. They're turned towards a makeshift stage, where a group of actors are dressed in costume. Some of the prisoners must be putting on a play. The lead actor is wearing a black top hat that's tall and crooked. He leans over a woman sleeping beneath a painted tree. His hands are held in front of him like claws, and his voice is high and piercing.

"And your family shall never know," he cries. "It is I who am the shaper of your dreams!"

He swishes his cape and laughs manically as he stalks off stage. The curtain comes down, and your eyes turn to the crowd. There are some prison guards there, but that shouldn't be a problem – they won't know who you are. So, squaring your shoulders, you start to make your way through from the back. Up on stage, the curtain rises. The man in the top hat stalks on, and draws back theatrically as someone strides to meet him. The newcomer is dressed in a soldier's uniform that barely covers his belly. He turns to the crowd and flings his arms wide.

"It is I, Edmund, come to reclaim my sister!"

There's a bored silence, and the man's face turns red as he embarks on his speech. But your attention is caught by a guard who's watching something behind you. Glancing over your shoulder, you see two town guards running your way. Someone must have seen you entering the grounds! You turn back to look at the empty expanse of grass beyond the stage. It lies between you and the woodland leading to Pendle Rise, and there's no way you could make it across without being seen. You'll have to create a distraction.

If you have the LAUGHING VAPOUR and would like to use it, turn to **31**.

If you have the SMOKE BOMB and would like to use it, turn to **364**.

If you have neither, or don't want to use them, turn to **145**.

77

Away from the tram, you hear the distant sirens of the Citadel. Guards will be spreading through the city, and when you see an alleyway you head straight for it. Ducking under some planks that are leaning across the entrance, you follow a dark channel between two decaying buildings. Cracked windows on one side, a damp wall on the other. You're entering the Doldrums. It's a dangerous part of town, but if there's one place you can hide from the guards, it's here.

After several minutes, you come to a courtyard that's probably never seen the sun. There's some graffiti showing Mayor Eldritch with her umbrella and top hat, a pair of horns emerging from under the brim. And in the opposite corner, some children are huddled together. You hear a tiny screech coming from their direction.

If you'd like to investigate, turn to **296**.

If you decide to carry on your way, turn to **194**.

78

The bomb disappears down its throat and you hear a dull thud. The mouth convulses as thick, black smoke billows out, and the long body writhes, sending waves sloshing over the embankment walls. With a low moan, the monster sinks back beneath the surface.

Gain 1 ABILITY point and delete the SMOKE BOMB from your LOG BOOK. Then turn to **188**.

79

You scrabble to unbuckle his sabre-belt – the fight must surely have alerted other guards. As you strap it around your waist, you look towards the cell and see the inmate, eyes glazed, staring at something only he can see. He's muttering to himself, the same four words: "the invaders are coming, the invaders are coming..." You sigh. Clearly you weren't going to get any sense out of him anyway. He starts whistling as you turn to leave, a short repetitive tune that follows you out of the chamber and lodges itself in your mind.

Make a note of the prisoner's tune in your LOG BOOK. There may be a time in your adventure where you'll want to try whistling it. If there is, then immediately turn back fifty entries. If the new entry doesn't make sense, go back to the entry you were on.

Also, add the NIGHT-SABRE to your LOG BOOK.

Turn to **305**.

80

Your sabre hangs limp by your side, your mind lost in a fog of memories. Some of them are your own, some aren't, but all of them are dark and cold. You hardly feel the bite of your opponent's sabre, as he brings down the final curtain.

81

You tell them she ran off, and ask to be let through to make your report to the warden. The second guard looks at the first, who nods reluctantly. They open the gates and let you pass.

Gain 1 ABILITY point, then turn to **76**.

82

You jump back behind the bow, and see the guards' carriage shake as their ballista fires. There's a brief moment when you think they've missed, then an even briefer moment when you realise they haven't.

Their bolt hits the diesel tank and ignites the fuel. It takes some time for them to find your body in the wreckage, with the water still pouring from the aqueduct above.

83

Your fist connects with his jaw and sends him down hard to the cobbles. He lies there for a moment, his eyes gradually focusing on the night-sabre held an inch from his nose, and in sullen silence he hands back your purse.

Breathing hard, you sheathe your sabre and turn to go. He waits until you've gone a safe distance, then calls out:

"I was a good worker before I stopped sleeping! I hope it happens to you – see what it's like!"

You walk on without looking back.

Turn to **162**.

84

The lock gives way easily and the door swings open. You step through and wedge it shut with a stack of luggage.

Turn to **33**.

85

People and buildings pass in a blur as the beast races through the streets. Your muscles scream and your arms are almost jerked from their sockets, but somehow you cling on until it starts to slow. You raise your head and see that you've entered a poor part of town called the Doldrums. If there's one place you can hide from the guards, it's here. In a quiet lane with no one about, you let go and slide to the ground. The creature hardly seems to notice and lumbers off down a side street.

Turn to **162**.

86

If you didn't drive the river monster back underwater, turn to **363** if you roll an odd double at any point in the fight (two 1s, two 3s or two 5s).

Rounds: 5   Damage: 2

YOU

If you win, turn to **282**.

If you lose, turn to **327**.

87

The last guard falls to the wet ground. You look up to see the passengers on the tram staring down open-mouthed. It's time you got off the main street.

Gain 1 ABILITY point, then turn to **77**.

88

The man sinks to his knees and you draw a deep, ragged breath. With shaking hands you pull the mirror from his grasp and hold it up to his face. A low moan escapes your lips.

"Who are you?" you whisper.

There's a gaping hole where his eye should be, and his lips are drawn back around long, metal teeth. At the end of each arm there are three dark night-sabres, growing from the hand like claws.

"You are Seagrave," the creature says, and the voice sounds like it's coming from the bottom of a deep well. "You are going to the

Citadel to find Eldritch. But you will never get there. The Order will be maintained."

The mouth opens impossibly wide, and an unearthly screech emerges. A warning signal not meant for human ears. And when you open your eyes the creature has gone, leaving only the clothes and the smell of brimstone behind.

The warning has been sounded, so until you're told otherwise, roll two DICE at the end of every new entry. Roll them **after** completing that entry, but **before** turning to the next one. If you roll a double, make a note of what entry you're on, then turn to **51**.

Now turn to **352**.

89

Fumbling in your bag, you find the bottle and uncork it. A strong, herbal smell fills the cave and the bear's nose twitches. You inch forwards until you can feel its warm breath on your face. The beast's eyes blink slowly and its mouth opens in a great yawn. This is your chance! You tip the contents down its throat and scramble away. The bear coughs and its eyes fly open. It sees you on the far side of the chamber and roars. How long does the potion take to work? You reach behind, frantically feeling for a way out, but there's only solid earth. Slowly, the beast rises. Its tongue flicks out to moisten its fangs. But then it grunts and stumbles forwards. Confusion clouds its eyes as it takes another unsteady step, before crashing to earth at your feet.

Looking up, you see a glimmer of light on the far side of the cave. It's the entrance, covered with branches and dead leaves. You tear them away and scramble back onto the path above.

Gain 1 ABILITY point, then turn to **356**.

90

Keeping those men in top hats in sight, you move slowly through the crowd. Your heartbeat pounds in your ears, every step feels like your last, but finally you make the entrance and don't look back. Gain 1 ABILITY point.

The way to the Field of Healing is one you've trodden many times as a guard, but you've never seen it so busy. You turn down a long stone passageway running inside the inner wall of the Citadel and find guards stationed at every post. Eldritch is taking no chances with this prisoner, whoever they are. Suddenly, you feel a heavy hand on your shoulder.

"Steady there, Seagrave," a voice whispers in your ear.

His other hand is on your sabre, preventing you from drawing, and you see the sleeve of a guard's uniform. Out loud, he orders you to come with him, and you're ushered into a small room off the main passageway. The door slams shut behind you, and only then can you turn. It takes you a moment to recognise him – it's Blake! The guard who slipped the key under the door of your cell.

"What are you doing here, Seagrave?"

He glares, and you stare back dumbly.

"I risked my life getting you out of this place!"

He pushes you in the chest and Meg pokes her head out and hisses. His broad shoulders rise and fall as he looks from her to you. His face is red and you take a step back. For a long moment you both stand frozen, and then his shoulders sag and he sits down heavily on a wooden bench.

"I picture you walking out of that gate every time another one dies."

He jabs a finger your way.

"You're the one I saved. Do you know how many I haven't?"

He looks down.

"I've lost count."

You sit next to him, and Meg climbs onto his lap. His great hand almost covers her. You tell him how you met Meg at Skerramore, and about the Watcher and Demon's Well. And the men in top hats and the mirror. You take it from your coat pocket to show him, but he holds his hand up to stop you.

"You haven't answered my question. I asked what you're doing *here*."

You look at him closely, suddenly wary.

If your SIXTH SENSE level is 6 or higher, turn to **318**.

If it's 5 or lower, turn to **214**.

91

The final guard falls with a sigh dying on his lips. He was younger than you. Wiping your sabre, you feel its cruel cold through the fabric of your sleeve.

At the end of the lane you meet one of Mirewick's many canals. Crossing over, you follow the towpath to the base of Pendle Rise. You've made it at last.

Turn to **221**.

92

His office overlooks the ground floor of the mill. You shut the door as he sits behind his desk and sifts through a pile of letters. You wonder what you're going to say, and glance around the room. There's a picture of Mayor Eldritch on the wall, and directly beneath the window, you see the hunched backs of the engine beasts. They've started using these creatures in place of steam engines in the factories, but this is the first time you've seen one. Three times the height of a man, they stand passively by their crankshafts and wait for the shift to start. It's no wonder the army uses them, too.

Suddenly the manager checks his watch and walks across to an odd contraption by the window. It looks like some kind of harmonium, but with symbols on the keys. He presses three of them down, and a strange noise fills the factory floor. It sounds like the song of a great, lost creature, and the effect on the engine beasts is immediate. As one, they bend their backs to the crankshafts and start turning. The floor shudders as the machines spring to life.

The manager sees your amazement.

"The perfect biological machines," he smiles. "Frighteningly strong, but with no will of their own. Complete slaves to the sounds in this box."

He pats the harmonium.

"Especially useful now that some workers have taken to those strange night-time walks that leave them good for nothing the next day. Now, what was your message?"

As you grasp for something that won't arouse suspicion, you look down and see a sudden commotion below. City guards are running through the door! One of them looks up and points your way. You can't hear what he's saying, but you can guess.

You draw your night-sabre. The manager backs up against the wall with his hands up, and you look wildly around the office. Your eyes settle on the harmonium.

Turn over to see it. The keys go from 1-9. Find the number for each key you want to press, going from left to right, then turn to the three-digit number you make. If you can't find the right number, turn to **157**.

93

A toot of the whistle spins you around.

"We're ready!" the woman cries.

Together you untie the lines and push the boat from the dock. With a last glance back up to the cottage, you step aboard.

"You should get below," she says, taking the tiller.

The cabin is warm and noisy from the engine next door. You light the lamp and sit on the small bed opposite the stove. From the porthole, you watch the warehouses slip by. Cliffs of red brick with loading bays five floors high. The old hoists hang damp and green.

"More coal for the engine," the woman calls, popping her head into the cabin. "And light the lamp on the bow."

"Why?" you ask, and she points down the canal. Sticking your head above the door, you see a dark tunnel approaching.

"Hurry," she says. "The ceiling's low."

Roll one DICE and add your ATHLETICISM level.

If your total is 7 or higher, turn to **268**.

If it's 6 or lower, turn to **358**.

94

The metal rails curve down the street and into Mirewick. Every second you expect the sirens to wail from the Citadel looming behind you. But at last, the tram approaches and comes to a stop in a cloud of steam. Lanterns sway outside the driver's cab as you climb aboard and buy a ticket. Deduct 1 SHILLING.

The carriage is filled with mill workers returning from the nightshift. There's only one seat free, next to a young woman wrapped in a shawl. She's fast asleep, with dark circles around her eyes. As the tram sets off, it begins to rain. Long rows of workers' houses pass by, their red bricks blackened by soot. Suddenly, there's a blast of the whistle, and the tram slows. You hear curses up ahead, but it's just a horse and cart on the wrong side of the street. The woman beside you stirs. Her eyelids blink open, and she looks at you in a daze.

"Where are we?" she murmurs, looking out the window. "I remember... no..."

She shakes her head and turns away. The tram's moving again, deeper into the city, past the pie merchants and barrow boys just setting out their stalls. The woman stands up to get off and you look down the road. Two guards are waiting by the next stop.

If you want to stay where you are and let them get on, turn to **272**.

If you want to jump off before the tram stops, turn to **131**.

If you want to force the driver to carry on without stopping, turn to **189**.

95

"It's true!" you cry, and tell him why you were arrested and how you escaped.

But your babble serves only to anger him further.

"Quiet!" he hisses. "You think you'd be spoutin' all that if it was true? For anyone to hear?"

He sweeps his arm towards the crowd.

"No, you're one of them."

Turn to **263**.

96

Orson raises his eyebrows and shakes his head.

"It's really not your lucky day, is it?"

If you want to accuse him of cheating, turn to **179**.

If you want to play again, turn to **217**.

If you'd like to leave, turn to **53**.

97

You force yourself to keep your pace slow and measured, but with every step you're expecting to hear the sirens wail from the Citadel on the hill. A woman behind you mutters to her companion.

"They arrested another one last night. Picked him up on Caxton Road. Raving, he was, so I've heard."

Her companion tuts.

"Sounds like nerves again, don't it? What's the trouble with people these days? They're going soft."

The first woman is quiet for a moment.

"My Arthur isn't sleeping," she says.

A couple of gaps in the crowd open up ahead of you.

Roll one DICE.

If you roll an even number, turn to **275**.

If you roll an odd number, turn to **321**.

98

The iron railings rise high above you, their ends viciously sharp. You follow them around, looking for a gap or a tree with an overhanging branch. But you find neither and wonder how much longer you should carry on looking.

Roll one DICE.

If you roll 1-3, turn to **234**.

If you roll 4-6, turn to **299**.

99

Their eyes are glazed and dull, and in the morning they'll probably have no memory of what they've done. But right now they fight like people trying to wake from a nightmare, and that makes them deadly. Your heel catches on a loose cobble and the woman is on you before your back hits the floor. She grabs your head and lifts it up, then suddenly stops. Her head turns. There's singing coming from across the square. A man stumbles over the cobbles singing a tuneless song. You see more sleepwalkers behind him, but he doesn't notice them until it's too late. The nearest two drag him to the ground, and the woman on your chest rushes across. She's forgotten all about you! Somehow, the man gets to his feet, his shirt ripped to the waist. Spinning around, wild-eyed, he tears down a side street.

Meg nips the skin beneath your shirt and it jolts you into action. This is your chance. You see the guard watching from the shadows of a dark lane and run across to join him.

Turn to **10**.

You nod.

"Just for a moment, then she shut them. Why?"

The younger imp spins around.

"It's not true! It's a big fib!"

Murmurs ripple through the circle.

"She's seen the lie," someone says, and others join in. "Yes, she's seen it."

She jabs her finger and glares through painted eyes.

"You keep quiet, Hob Gadlin! You're just after my cooking pots."

But the white-haired imp cuts her off and gestures to someone in the circle.

"Silly girl. Take her away."

Deduct 1 ABILITY point.

You scrabble to rescue the situation, say that maybe you were mistaken, but you struggle to be heard above the insults flying back and forth.

"I see you peeking at the station every time a train comes in!"

"How would you know, Ivy? You peeking too?"

Two imps grab Ivy, the one you chased, and you reach for your sabre. But suddenly the old imp raises her cane, and everyone falls quiet.

"You see how the dreamless ones muddy the stream?" she cries. "We must stay pure."

The circle parts and a team of imps enter, dragging some kind of ogre into the firelight. The beast is a head taller than you, and its white skin is covered in intricate, swirling tattoos of red and gold. There's a blindfold over its eyes.

"Leave us be, Dreamless One," the old imp calls. "Or we'll remove the blindfold."

If you want to fight the ogre, turn to **290**.

If not, turn to **252**.

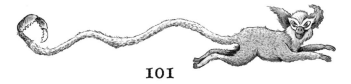

101

Because you're fighting without a weapon, you must subtract 1 from each dice roll. For example, if you roll for 7 or more to do 1 damage, you must roll 8 or more to be successful.

PICKPOCKET

Rounds: 5   Damage: 1

YOU

If you win, turn to **83**.

If you lose, turn to **161**.

102

"On second thoughts," you say, "I think I'll take my business elsewhere."

You push the luggage aside and step back outside.

"So that's how you got on," she calls. "You'd better jump, or you'll have to pay for the door."

Roll one DICE.

If you roll an even number, turn to **243**.

If you roll an odd number, turn to **68**.

103

She looks disappointed.

"Oh, you called it right. That means I'm in a gentle, loving mood."

She frowns, then brightens and bows theatrically.

"You may go."

Impatiently you brush past. The strange woman, really more of a girl, is still bowed low. But suddenly she sticks her cane out and sends you sprawling.

"Is there a present for little Evie?" she asks. "Just to say thanks for not hurting you?"

If you decide to pay her, choose any one item, except for your NIGHT-SABRE, and delete it from your LOG BOOK. Then turn to **49**.

If you choose not to, turn to **279**.

104

"Open up!"

The shout comes first, then a bang at the door that rattles the windowpanes.

Darting across, you peek through a chink in the curtains.

"Guards!" you whisper.

But she's already at the back door, waving you across. You follow down a steep flight of steps and see the canal below. There's a narrowboat moored on the dock, painted bright red and green. She throws open the hatch to the engine room and you hear a crash from the cottage above.

"I need to fire up the boiler!" she shouts. "You'll have to hold them off!"

The first guard appears in the doorway.

If you have the MINIATURE CROSSBOW and would like to use it, turn to **172**.

If you don't, turn to **215**.

105

You feel your hold on reality slipping. The man's face fades, a smile playing on his pale lips, and memories flicker through your mind. Your time as a cadet, long days on the beat, Malory's whisper and the following night, when they dragged you from your room and threw you in the tower.

And then the man in the top hat finds what he's looking for. The conversation with the Watcher, her picture on the wall. Skerramore.

You dimly feel Meg scrambling up your chest, leaping with a screech that turns to a whimper, and when you wake, the man is gone, replaced by a compartment full of guards. Out of the window you see the Citadel looming above the blackened streets of Mirewick. They're taking you back to the Field of Healing, where your journey ends.

106

If this is the first time you've turned to this entry, turn to **213**.
If it's the second time, turn to **66**.

107

You tell him you're no friend of the guards.

"Those sirens are for me," you gasp. "I should be dead already."

"What do you mean?" he says. "You think I believe that?"

Roll one DICE and add your SIXTH SENSE level.

If your total is 7 or higher, turn to **210**.

If it's 6 or lower, turn to **95**.

108

As the panting of the tram recedes, you hear the distant sirens of the Citadel. Guards will be spreading through the city – you need to get off the main street. Looking around, you see a lane lined with tall, grim-looking buildings. It leads into a dangerous part of town called the Doldrums, but it's your only choice. You pass pawnbrokers' shops with faded signs and dusty displays. A woman tries to sell you vegetables from a basket slung across her chest, and up above grey faces seem to thrust like gargoyles from every window. In the doorway of a tavern, a workman leans with his paper hat cocked so you can see only one beady eye. It watches you approach, and he walks across as you draw near.

"Anything I can help you with, officer?" he says. "We don't often see your illustrious sort down this way. At least, not on your own."

You smile politely and carry on past, but he chases after you.

"You're missing out, you know, just hurrying through like this. There's plenty of hidden talents in these parts."

He leaps in front of you and spreads his arms wide.

"Take me for instance."

You gasp. Your purse dangles from his right hand. A small crowd has gathered, and they wait to see what you'll do.

If you want to try to snatch it back, turn to **71**.

If you decide to push past without it, turn to **8**.

If you'd like to wait and see what he says, turn to **239**.

109

You decide you have more pressing concerns than haggling over the price. The old lady gives a big, shiny grin as you pay the money and take the cloak.

Deduct 3 SHILLINGS and add the CLOAK to your LOG BOOK. Then turn to **198**.

110

The rows of houses stretch away on either side. Distant cries disturb the silence, and a cat runs across your path, disappearing down a dark lane. Suddenly you hear footsteps. A guard races onto the street. He turns, and his face is lit by the lamp above. He's panting hard, fear in his eyes.

"Help me!" he calls.

But before you can reply he looks back down the lane and cries out. Two men in top hats emerge. The guard tries to run, but his movements are suddenly slow, as if he's fighting against an invisible current. He clutches his head and moans.

If you'd like to help the guard, turn to **18**.

If not, turn to **385**.

III

The bomb flies past the monster's mouth and lands in the river with an apologetic splosh.

Delete the SMOKE BOMB from your LOG BOOK, then turn to **188**.

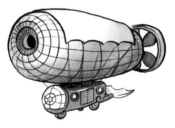

112

You launch yourself forwards to tackle the guard before he can draw his weapon. But you're a fraction late and he scrambles to his feet, night-sabre in hand. It grazes the low ceiling and your eyes meet. The cramped space gives you a chance, and there's one thing he probably doesn't know – you were trained in hand-to-hand combat as an elite guard.

Because you don't have a weapon, you must subtract 1 from each dice roll. For example, if you roll for 7 or more to do 1 damage, you must roll 8 or more to be successful.

Rounds: 6

Damage: 1

YOU

If you win, turn to **175**.

If you lose, turn to **288**.

113

Jonas staggers and drops his cane. You help him to the ground as a drop of blood trickles from the corner of his mouth. He dabs it with a white hanky.

"You do me a service, my friend," he gasps. "If I'd lived much longer I'd have become one of *them*."

You ask if he means a sleepwalker and he nods.

"I may be losing my wits, but I haven't lost them yet."

He winces in pain.

"Oh, by the way, that execution is this morning," he whispers. "Looks like you might be able to make it after all."

You smile grimly. So, now you know where things will end, one way or the other. The place you've been running from all this time. The Field of Healing.

Turn to **38**.

114

You try to run along the wooden sleepers of the track, but your stride is slightly off and the loose gravel slows you down. If you don't catch the rear carriage soon, your chance will be lost. With a final effort you close the gap and leap for the back step.

Roll one DICE.

If you roll 1-3, turn to **11**.

If you roll 4-6, turn to **383**.

115

Fresh pies are cooling on the counter, alongside a big pot of tea. The woman looks at you again, and you pretend to fumble in your bag for money. She turns to serve another customer. This is your chance.

Roll one DICE and add it to your SKILL level.

If your total is 9 or higher, turn to **271**.

If it's 8 or lower, turn to **320**.

116

The air is warm, heated by a steaming cauldron in the centre of the tent. You scan the benches and see no guards. It costs one shilling for a bowl of stew and a mug of tea.

If you'd like to buy a meal, turn to **273**.

If you don't have the money, but would like to ask for a meal, turn to **384**.

If you want to leave the tent, turn to **201**.

You realise you're whistling that woman's tune. Except it's not hers, is it? You've heard it once before. But where? It seems important. You glance down at the newspaper, at the story of the arrest, and gasp. The mad prisoner in the tower. It was his tune! You spin around, looking for the woman. It's probably nothing, but it's such an odd little tune... You catch a glimpse of her leaving the square and take off in pursuit. She turns down a passageway and slows as you call out. You pause to catch your breath, then whistle the tune. Slowly, she turns around.

"Yes?"

Her eyes flicker to the guard's badge and her mouth tightens.

"What do you want?"

You say you heard what she was whistling. That you've heard it before, in the tower. She looks at you in silence, arms crossed. A few strands of grey hair have slipped from under her bonnet, and you realise she's waiting for something. Your shoulders slump.

"I'm not a guard," you say. "Not anymore. I was arrested for something a prisoner said to me. Not him in the tower, somebody else. And I don't know why."

The words come tumbling out. All the confusion and fear and anger that you've had no time to feel until now.

"But that man who whistled the tune, I thought he might be the one you were reading about. He said something... something about an invasion." You laugh and trail off, realising how ridiculous you sound.

"It doesn't matter," you mutter.

She catches your arm as you turn to go.

"Come with me," she says.

Gain 2 ABILITY points, then turn to **63**.

118

It's the screech that tears you from your stupor. Small, high-pitched and desperate. Meg is hanging over the pot, tied to a pole, and the old lady has her hooked tail in one hand and a cleaver in the other!

"We'll have no more of that, my little imp," she mutters, raising the blade.

You cry out, your words slurred, and she whirls around with surprising speed. Except it's not quite her. The eyes are white and blind and the teeth are too large for her jaws. They glint in the firelight, long and rusted. They look like they're made of iron.

"Ah," she says sweetly. "The main course."

She tosses the cleaver aside and leaps across the floor in a single bound. You tumble back out of your chair and her long, yellow claws graze your neck. Deduct 1 LIFE point. Scrabbling to your feet, you draw your night-sabre.

WITCH

Rounds: 5   Damage: 2

YOU

If you win, turn to **143**.

If you lose, turn to **370**.

119

"It's daylight robbery!" you say, trying to push through the crowd.

It's the excuse several of them have been waiting for. They're on you in a flash, pinning your arms to the ground before you can reach for your night-sabre. A gag is forced into your mouth, and you watch helplessly as they discuss what to do with you. Someone mentions the guards' station nearby.

"But he's a guard himself!" another says. "They won't do anything."

Just then, as if on cue, the sirens wail from the citadel wall. You stiffen, and the old lady studies you shrewdly.

"I wouldn't be so sure," she says, and gives a grin that reveals a top row of silver teeth.

Your execution takes place the same day.

120

Madame Esther counts down and pulls the card from the deck. She lays it beside the other two and mutters an incantation under her breath. But the light in the crystal starts to fade, the mists return and disperse. The ball is empty and lifeless.

"What happened?" you ask, looking up.

Esther sighs and hides the ball under the cloth once more.

"Nothing, Seagrave. Because you chose the wrong card."

You want to ask her how she knows your name, but her face is cold and set. She picks up the cards and shuffles them into the deck.

"You can go," she says, without looking up. "The coast is clear."

Deduct 1 ABILITY point, then turn to **303**.

121

Using the hook as a foothold, you swing your legs over and gently slide down the other side. After putting it back in your bag, you set off through the grounds.

Turn to **76**.

122

As the sky brightens, the sleepwalkers wake. They look down at their torn clothes and start running home before anyone sees them. The Citadel is close now, and soon you're joined in the street by the early risers. Some going to work, some to the execution, no doubt. A pie shop has opened early and has a board outside advertising 'Hangman's Hogget'. Your stomach growls and you realise how long it's been since your last meal.

If you'd like to pop into the shop, turn to **369**.

If you decide not to, turn to **177**.

123

Your mouth falls open in disbelief as the spinner seems to slow suddenly and land on the one.

Orson turns to the crowd with a theatrical shrug.

"You wouldn't believe it if you hadn't just seen it with your own eyes, ladies and gentlemen."

He sighs.

"I'm a grizzled old showman, but I have a heart."

He takes a single shilling from his purse and presents it with a flourish.

"Here's the shilling back that began this sorry episode. Take it, to ward off any more bad luck."

The crowd gives an appreciative murmur.

If you want to accuse him of cheating, turn to **195**.

If you'd like to take the shilling and leave, turn to **311**.

124

"SHREEKERS!"

You sit bolt upright, and the hammock tips you onto the deck.

"Get up here," Gambrel shouts.

Scrambling to your feet you run to the helm. The mountains are sharp and jagged on the horizon. Almost blinding in the morning sun. You shield your eyes and see a ragged band of birds above the ridgeline.

"They're not birds," Gambrel growls. "And they'll tear my ship apart."

He points back into the centre of the cabin.

"Under that canvas. It's a turret. Sit down and I'll drop you through."

You drag away the canvas and stand back. It's a giant crossbow. The bolts alone are the length of your arm, fed into the groove along a leather belt. And behind is a seat with a harness attached. It's only then that Gambrel's words register.

"Drop me through...?"

"Strap in, Seagrave! There's pedals to swivel you round. It's them or us!"

You don't have time to think. There are goggles on the seat, and you strap in. Your stomach lurches as he drops you through the cabin floor, and the noise from the propeller is deafening. It takes a moment to get your bearings. Then you see them. Their giant, bat-like wings beating in unison – they're almost upon you! Gambrel brings the ship about and they flash past with an unearthly screech, their long claws inches from the thin skin that's keeping you aloft. You swivel the turret and watch them turn.

There are twelve bolts in your bow as you line the first shreeker up in your sights.

... Roll one DICE.

Roll a 6: you kill it – fill in both halves of its crossbones.

Roll a 4 or 5: you wound it – fill in one half of its crossbones.

Roll a 1, 2 or 3: you miss.

If your SKILL level is 5 or higher, add 1 to each roll. For example, a 3 becomes a 4.

When both halves of the creatures' crossbones are filled in, they tumble from the sky. After each roll, scribble out one of your twelve bolts below.

SHREEKER   SHREEKER

SHREEKER

If you kill all three shreekers before running out of bolts, turn to **331**.

If you don't, turn to **376**.

125

A fisher lands on your neck and latches on with its sharp little teeth. As you slither over the wet cobbles, you tear it off and fling it against the wall. The end of the passageway jolts and blurs in your vision. You feel them on your back, around your feet, and then you slip and they're swarming all over you. Their screeches fill your ears. You stagger up and stumble the last few paces onto a wide square. Finally, the fishers melt back into the shadows. Breathing hard, you look around you.

Deduct 2 LIFE points and turn to **43**.

126

Blake blows his whistle, trying to rally more guards to the stage, and you remember the whistle in your coat pocket. You put it to your lips. The note is strange, almost like a living thing, and the gold rune on its side starts to glow. You hear something, faint at first, but getting louder, stronger. A voice within.

"Ahhhh... There you are, at lassst."

You almost drop the whistle to the floor. You think it's talking to you, but Eldritch has drawn back, as if stung. You hear her voice inside your head.

"I thought you'd have rotted away in prison by now, Hezrach."

The whistle pulses between your fingers as a laugh turns to a wail.

"Soon... soon. But your old mentor couldn't go without leaving you a parting gift."

And suddenly the whistle starts to vibrate so fast that you drop it to the floor. It glows white hot, and a sound emerges that goes beyond human hearing. Eldritch's staff explodes in her hands, and with a soft sigh, the whistle turns to dust.

Eldritch is still for a moment, then she rears up to her full height and turns towards you.

Turn to **278**.

127

"The invaders, Seagrave. The invaders."

Deduct 1 ABILITY point, then turn to **159**.

128

The cat is already out of reach. You look up and see the green eyes of the fisher high on a ledge. Casting around, you grab an empty bottle and throw it.

Roll one DICE and add your SKILL level.

If your total is 8 or higher, turn to **25**.

If it's 7 or lower, turn to **230**.

129

The trees thin out as you near the summit. It's late afternoon and the sky is deep blue. There's a short scramble up loose rocks and then you're over the crest. In front is a small, frozen lake. The wind slices through your clothing and blows flurries of snow over the ice. High above, a bird wheels. There's nothing here. Nothing at all. You pick up a stone and launch it over the lake. It slides across and drops out of sight. You stare for a moment. Must be a trick of the light. You pick your way around to where the stone should be, and there you see them. Steps. Steps cut down through the rock.

"She was right, Meg," you whisper. "I'm not going crazy."

She climbs out onto your shoulder. The steps are narrow and steep, and soon you're feeling your way through darkness with your hands on the cold walls. Finally, you see a glimmer of light ahead. The left wall drops away and the stone steps spiral down the inside of a great, hollow chamber. Blue light streams through the frozen lake that hangs suspended above your head. There are pictures carved into the rockface, and as you pass, they show tales of ancient battles and fearsome monsters. Below, you see the light waver. There's water down there, dark and smooth. A narrow walkway leads into the centre of the chamber, to a column that rises above the pool. And at the top of the column there's a narrow slot. The Watcher's words come like a whisper: '*Take the looking glass to Demon's Well*'. Slowly, carefully, you pull it from your coat pocket.

Yes, the handle is a perfect fit. You push it into the slot and step back. Meg shifts nervously on your shoulder, and you see two points of light below, getting larger, brighter. The water beneath you quivers and starts to frost over. Suddenly, this doesn't feel a safe place to stand.

Roll one DICE and add your ATHLETICISM level.

If your total is 9 or higher, turn to **225**.

If it's 8 or lower, turn to **16**.

130

Too late the lightning flashes, too late you see the white cliffs of the jagged peak, rising high above the rest. There's just time to see Gambrel spin the wheel, to feel Meg's claws dig into your side. And then your ship strikes the rock and goes up like a match, before breaking apart on the slopes below.

131

You decide it's not worth the risk. Moving quickly to the back of the carriage, you wait for a tree to hide you from view, then jump down onto the street.

If your ATHLETICISM level is 4 or higher, turn to **26**.

If it's 3, turn to **153**.

132

As you snatch at thin air, there's a roar of laughter from the crowd. The man bows theatrically.

Turn to **239**.

133

The crowd scatters as you leap up on stage. Orson sidesteps your lunge and puts the spinner between you.

"Help!" he cries. "The guard's gone mad!"

You chase him around the wheel, with his red waistcoat always just out of reach. In the end, you haul the spinner to the ground.

"Got you now!" you snarl.

Orson backs away, but suddenly a grin spreads across his face.

"Afraid not," he replies.

You look around and see you're surrounded by guards. How could you have lost sight of why you were cutting through the fair in the first place?

"It's really not your day, is it?" Orson calls, as you're dragged from the stage.

Your execution takes place the following morning.

134

Blake's fist fills your vision and then all you see is stars.

"You idiot!" he hisses. "How can you not trust me when I got you out of here in the first place?"

You wipe a trickle of blood from your lip.

"Now get this animal off me!"

You call Meg away and he stands opposite you, breathing heavily.

Deduct 1 LIFE point, then turn to **180**.

135

"Your dreams, Seagrave, and the dreams of all Mirewick. Every night, they flow into the Citadel, and we feast until you have nothing left to give."

"And what happens then?" you ask. "To the people with nothing left."

"Ah," she says. "The sleepwalkers. Yes, some people can't cope for long without their dreams. It *is* unfortunate."

You stop still on the thick red carpet.

"Unfortunate?"

"But surely you see, my sweet, sentimental Seagrave. Surely you wouldn't want us to starve?"

For a moment there's silence. And then you hear music. Faint, far off. It sounds like a fairground organ. It sounds, somehow, like hope.

"What's that?" Eldritch asks, her voice suddenly sharp.

On the wall, the lamps flicker, and you follow the sound until you come to a set of stairs that weren't there before.

"Stop!" Eldritch cries. "Don't go down there."

Now it's your turn to laugh. You look along the empty, endless corridor, and think about your neck on the block. The axe.

"I don't think I've got much to lose," you say.

The stairs lead to a dimly lit lounge. There's a bar on the far side, and the barman beckons. As you make your way between the tables, you see a wooden dummy in every chair. In silence, their heads swivel to watch you pass. And then you see it's not drinks behind the bar at all, it's a fairground game. The organ music starts up once more and the dummies laugh, their empty mouths hanging open.

"Oh look! Oh look!"

There's a high, nasal voice, and you see a puppet at the end of the bar. He's sitting by a telegraph machine. It springs to life with a series of rapid clicks.

"It's a message from the Outside!" he says.

Eldritch screams with rage and the clicking suddenly stops. Smoke rises from the machine.

"Now look what she's done," the puppet says sadly.

The dummies laugh, and the barman tilts his head.

"Hard luck," he says. "But why not have a game anyway?"

He leans forwards and the shadows fall across his face.

"What have you got to lose?"

Turn over to see the game, and if you can work out how to win the game, turn to the entry you find.

If you choose incorrectly, turn to 2.

136

The line north to the Whistling Mountains runs along the far side of Pendle Rise. There the trains slow down enough for you to try hopping aboard to avoid any guards that could be waiting at the station.

If you want to try train-hopping, turn to **182**.

If you'd prefer to go to the station, turn to **373**.

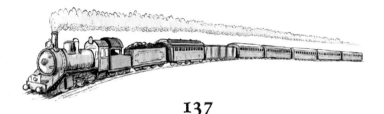

137

Climbing through the forest, you see nothing but trees and snow. Maybe from the top you'll find whatever it is you're looking for. But the going is tough, and you find yourself wading through deep drifts and splashing across icy streams. You come to the mouth of a ravine.

If you'd like to go through the ravine, turn to **186**.

If you'd like to avoid the ravine by going right, turn to **382**.

If you'd like to avoid the ravine by going left, turn to **22**.

138

You hesitate. Should you tell them the truth, that there was a fight between the two of you?

If your SIXTH SENSE level is 5 or higher, turn to **357**.

If it's 4 or lower, turn to **254**.

139

The guard beside you fights like a man possessed, but his cries fade as the men in top hats flood your mind with darkness. Your arms hang limp as he finally falls, and you sink to your knees. Meg climbs up onto your shoulder and screeches, small and fierce. With the last of your strength you tell her to run, but she screeches again and again – and suddenly it seems like there are screeches all around. Something soft brushes past your face. There's a hiss of rage and your eyes fly open. There are fishers everywhere! Leaping and biting and tearing, and as the men in top hats flail you stagger to your feet and cut them down. Then silence, as the fishers melt back into the dark streets.

Meg gives a satisfied chirp, and in spite of everything, you grin.

"I'd like to see them try getting inside your head," you say. "They wouldn't know what hit them."

And then, with a deep breath, you turn back towards the Citadel. Turn to **122**.

140

You step up to the hatch and slide it open. The man inside rushes over, his face swollen and bruised. He looks at you, then past you, and puts his fingers to his lips. It's only then that you hear the bootsteps coming up behind. There's no time to hide. The guard appears at the entrance to the chamber and his hand flies to his night-sabre.

If your ATHLETICISM level is 4, turn to **339**.

If it's 3, turn to **112**.

141

You reach desperately for the banister as your knees buckle. Your fingers clasp the handrail and you cling on, waiting for the room to stop spinning. At the bottom of the stairs the butler pulls out a chair. You stumble down, take a seat and close your eyes.

Turn to **248**.

142

You realise Ada is shouting. She seems far away.

"Up! Up!"

Without stopping to think, you stumble up the steps. The men in top hats are running down the embankment, and you look back towards the river. The water is calm and smooth. Everything is suddenly quiet. Ada claps you on the back.

"You're tougher than you look, Seagrave. They ran when that one you were fighting went down."

You ask who they were and she shrugs.

"I don't know. But they're after the sleepwalkers and we try to stop them."

She looks you up and down and smiles.

"So, they didn't get you then."

"What do you mean?"

"It's been months since I saw you. Where have you been? Did you find anything at Skerramore?"

You stare.

"Months?"

"Must be. Seems like a lifetime, doesn't it?"

She mistakes your silence for agreement and shakes her head. "Feels like things are falling apart."

You realise now why the guard didn't recognise you. Somehow you've arrived back in Mirewick months after you left! This must be the moment the dragon was talking about. But what's happened to the place?

Turn to **308**.

143

The witch thrashes around on the floor, a foul-smelling grey fluid seeping through her white dress until finally she lies still, her metal teeth locked in a crazed grin. Stepping gingerly over the body, you free Meg from the pole. She chatters furiously and runs across, but when you turn, the witch has gone! There's just a steaming pile of clothes where she lay, and the smell of brimstone fills the cottage. Rushing outside, you breathe the cold, fresh air.

"Meg!" you call. "Let's get out of here."

She jumps onto your shoulder, and together you hurry away from the cottage and up the mountain.

Gain 1 ABILITY point, then turn to **356**.

144

The third guard looks at the two bodies lying between you and him, then he looks up towards the door. You take a step forwards, and he bolts for the cottage. You've held them off, for now!

Turn to **93**.

You need to make a disturbance that won't centre on you. Looking left and right, you search desperately for inspiration. And then you see it. Fat, brown and waddling past your boot. A toad!

Up on stage, Edmund is striking a heroic pose. You didn't hear his speech, but you don't think much of the crowd did either. They look bored and restless. Ready for some excitement. You pick up the toad and wait for the town guards to start moving through the crowd, then launch it towards the stage.

Roll one DICE and add your SKILL level.

If your total is 7 or higher, turn to **208**.

If it's 6 or lower, turn to **191**.

146

Something tells you the guard isn't just asleep on his watch. You pick up the bottle and take a sniff. There's a strange undercurrent there – subtle, but bitter. He'll be asleep for a good while yet.

Gain 1 ABILITY point and turn to **260**.

147

You shake your head. Gain 1 ABILITY point.

"No," you say. "Her eyes were shut. I didn't expect to see anyone out here. I'm climbing the mountain."

There's a sudden disturbance in the circle.

"Sacrilege!" someone shouts, but the old imp raises her arms once more.

"Quiet!" she cries, before turning back to you. "And what is it you seek, Dreamless One?"

Turn to **36**.

148

He disappears down a side street and you wonder what he was running from. Then someone drifts onto the square. She moves with a strange, aimless air, and two more follow. A man and a woman. Their steps are slow and heavy, as if they're half-asleep. They look up. Their faces are blank and hollow-eyed, but now they're moving quickly, running straight for you with their arms flailing and teeth bared!

You have no choice but to fight them, but your attackers give little thought to fighting as a group, so if you lose a round, only count the damage from the one you chose to target. If you win the round, only deduct the COMBAT points from that attacker, too. And remember also to keep a note of how many rounds you have left for that opponent.

FIRST SLEEPWALKER

Rounds: 5   Damage: 1

SECOND SLEEPWALKER

Rounds: 3   Damage: 2

THIRD SLEEPWALKER

Rounds: 3   Damage: 1

YOU

If you win, turn to **203**.

If you lose, turn to **99**.

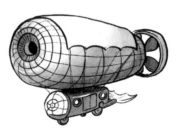

149

The crowd is packed tightly together and the going is tough.

If your ENDURANCE level is 4 or higher, turn to **368**.

If it's 3, turn to **312**.

150

With an apologetic shrug, you draw your sabre and say you haven't got the time to waste. Slowly, he tucks the cards into his shirt pocket and looks up.

"Well, I'll make this quick, then."

He leans down and whispers to the dog. It almost knocks the table over in its eagerness to get to your throat.

GUARD DOG

Rounds: 2   Damage: 2

YOU

♡ ♡ ♡ ♡ ♡ ♡ ♡ ♡ ♡ ♡ ♡ ♡

If you win, turn to **338**.

If you lose, turn to **20**.

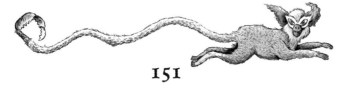

151

She scowls and cuffs you over the head.

"Haven't you been listening? I've no idea who they are, or why they're attacking the sleepwalkers. Or how they get inside your head and make it so you just lie down and let them finish you off."

Deduct 1 ABILITY point.

If you want to ask another question, turn to **308**.

If you want to get on your way, turn to **365**.

152

You follow the fence around until you're hidden from the gate by trees. The railings rise above you, tall and viciously sharp. Taking the grappling hook from your bag, you sling it over and pull it back until it catches. You test your weight and start to climb, eyeing the spikes at the top warily.

Roll one DICE and add your ATHLETICISM level.

If your total is 8 or higher, turn to **121**.

If it's 7 or lower, turn to **245**.

153

You're caught out by the speed you're travelling and fall sideways onto the wet cobbles.

Deduct 1 LIFE point, then turn to **77**.

154

You run back up the stairs, gripping the key tightly. Which way to Room 187? You look left and right. The door numbers aren't in order! And then the lamps go out and you can't see any numbers at all. Eldritch's laugh creeps through the darkness.

"So sorry, Seagrave. Must be a problem with the gas supply."

In desperation, you feel your way along the corridor, using your fingers to trace the numbers on the doors. It's useless. You'll never find it like this. But suddenly a lone light flares, far off down the corridor. You run towards it and Eldritch screams in fury. The walls and floor start to shake horribly, and behind you the corridor is falling away, disappearing into darkness like it's trying to swallow you up. You reach the door. 187. The key turns with a click, and you fall through into the room beyond.

Turn to **378**.

155

Without realising it, Ada gave you a pendant that protects its wearer from dark magic. But you see its power is limited. The attack has left the stone tarnished and dulled – it will only be able to save you from one more black magic attack.

Turn to the end of the **previous entry**.

156

You look across and see the concentration on his face as he tries to resume control. You focus on his face, focus on staying in the compartment, and feel the fingers of your hand twitch. He redoubles his efforts, and the memories rise up once more.

This is a battle like any other, but because the fight is taking place without weapons, you must subtract 1 from each dice roll. For example, if you roll for 7 or more to do 1 damage, you must roll 8 or more to be successful.

MAN IN TOP HAT

Rounds: 3   Damage: 2

YOU

If you win, turn to **359**.

If you lose, turn to **105**.

157

Desperately you press key after key as the guards mount the stairs. You're still pressing them as they walk through the door. The manager suddenly regains his courage.

"He's over there," he says, with a dismissive wave of his hand.

You're bound and transported back to the Citadel, where your execution takes place towards evening.

158

He beckons you to follow, and the dog growls as you edge around the table. Meg pops her head out of your coat and chatters back. The boy looks at you in surprise, but carries on to the back of the cellar, where a long rack of dusty bottles reaches up to the ceiling. Grasping two of the struts, he slides them apart to reveal a hidden door.

"Ready?" he says.

He lights a lamp and leads you down into a network of dark passageways and forgotten cellars.

"We've found all sorts down here," he murmurs, looking over his shoulder. "Weapons, maps... strange writings."

His voice tails off and you ask what he means.

"Just ravings I suppose, about an invasion, hidden forces. Some of it was hard to read, like they were losing their mind... I don't read them anymore."

You ask why not.

"Because of the sleepwalkers. It's like it's happening again."

In a large chamber you see rows and rows of beds filled with children. Some of them are asleep, others watch you pass, clutching a favourite toy.

"Orphans," he says. "Some sleepwalkers never wake up... It's safer down here for those left behind."

One of the children cries out in their sleep, and anger wells up inside you. Eldritch will pay for what she's done. You promise yourself this.

Eventually the boy stops and puts his ear to a doorway.

"This is as far as I can get you. The Citadel is just over the way."

You nod your thanks, and he presses something into your hand. A brown paper package.

"Breakfast," he says with a smile. "You look like you could use it."

As the door closes, you polish off a jam sandwich and a bottle of ginger ale.

Add 3 LIFE points, then turn to **177**.

159

"They didn't come for land or riches. They came to feast on our dreams. That's how they live. And they walk among us, hidden in plain sight while the world crumbles around them."

You open your mouth, but the dragon continues.

"No one can live without their dreams forever, Seagrave. You will see things when you return..."

It looks up at the light streaming in from above.

"First people lose their dreams, then they lose their minds. That is why Eldritch must be stopped."

The voice is so faint now that you can hardly hear it.

"You have one chance to defeat her, Seagrave. Just one moment in time."

You ask what you must do, and a ghostly claw points to the lake below.

"You jump. The lake will take you to that moment."

You look down and see stars in the water. And a clocktower, stretching up to the night sky. It's Mirewick.

Turn to **257**.

160

You look down and see your night-sabre halfway out of its sheath. There's a hook under the handle, lifting it gently into the air. Jumping back, you hear a hiss and a screech as a fisher falls from a windowsill above the door! It leaps to its feet and disappears inside the house.

Turn to **294**.

161

A lifetime of street brawling proves more than a match for your guard's training. You strain to break free and reach for your night-sabre, but his tattooed forearms have you trapped in a vice-like hold.

"Not so easy without your friends, is it?" he whispers, so close that you feel his hot breath in your ear.

If you want to tell him you're no longer a guard, turn to **107**.

If you'd prefer to keep quiet, turn to **263**.

162

The lane twists and turns and takes you deeper into the Doldrums. Rainwater starts to trickle down your back. Then from a small side-alley you hear yowling and turn to see a cat being hoisted into the air. It flails about, caught on a single, hooked claw gripping its soft belly. It's been caught by a fisher! These creatures come from foreign lands, but have learnt to thrive in the dark alleyways of Mirewick. On the end of their long, black tails they have a sharp claw, which they hang perfectly still, waiting for cats or rats to pass by.

If you'd like to help the cat, turn to **128**.

If you decide to carry on down the lane, turn to **334**.

163

Slowly, lazily, the bear moves forwards. Its bulk seems to fill the cave. You feint one way then the other, but the back of the bear's paw smashes you against the wall. Your breath comes in ragged gasps as you see the entrance just to your right. Tearing at the branches, you feel a claw dig deep into your thigh.

Deduct 4 LIFE points, then turn to **200**.

164

You land between its shoulder blades and grab the chain around its neck. The beast roars and you cling on for dear life as it lurches across the room. Its foul sweat soaks through your clothing and stings your eyes. You don't even realise it's heading for a window until you hear the crash, and then it's pounding over cobbles and vaulting a low wall.

Roll one DICE and add your ATHLETICISM and ENDURANCE levels.

If your total is 10 or higher, turn to **85**.

If it's 9 or lower, turn to **330**.

165

He relaxes a little in the cosy confines of the kitchen and tells you there are no other staff, except for a gardener who comes occasionally.

"I can't tell you how many times I've looked at that picture," he says, buttering two thick slices of bread. "I don't *stare*, just a quick glance while dusting or walking past. I'm never sure whether she can see out, you see."

As he walks across to the pantry, a hooked tail descends from the ceiling and takes a slice of bread. He returns with a block of cheese.

"I know someone who's not getting their hot water bottle

tonight," he says loudly, cutting another slice of bread.

A crust bounces off his head.

"And that's the first time I've heard her talk, or seen her move, in all my years working here."

You ask him how long that is, and he tells you he's been the butler of Skerramore since his dad died thirty years ago.

"And *he* never saw her either. You have to go back eight generations to find an Arkwright who waited on my lady in the flesh."

He puts the sandwich down in front of you.

"She's really that old?"

He nods.

"She's been waiting a long time."

Add 3 LIFE POINTS, then turn to **380**.

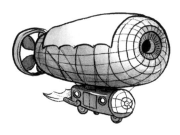

166

Without realising it, Ada gave you a pendant that protects its wearer from dark magic. But overcoming this man has drained all its power. For a moment it glows bright, then it crumbles to dust in your hand.

Delete the PENDANT from your LOG BOOK, then turn to the end of the **previous entry**.

167

You're sitting next to a woman in a brown woollen dress and a yellow bonnet. She's bent over an article in the newspaper, tracing the lines with her finger and mouthing the words. You clasp your hands around your mug and listen to two men talking behind you. "It's still on the loose," one of them is saying. "Smashed through a window at the mill and never looked back."

"What do they expect?" his companion mutters. "Putting those beasts to work alongside women and children..."

"'Scuse me, love." The woman has stood up to leave. Your eyes meet, and you make room as she squeezes past, whistling a short, repetitive tune under her breath.

You glance over the story she was reading. It's about a man who was arrested for disrupting a speech given by Mayor Eldritch at the city hall, yelling something about an invasion. You drain your mug and leave the tent.

There are many routes to Pendle Rise, but two that seem best.

If you'd like to make your way through a rich area filled with big townhouses, turn to **316**.

If you'd like to cut through the grounds of Mirewick's largest prison, turn to **39**.

168

The memories flash through your mind's eye until you can no longer see who you're fighting. Then new images appear. Not your own memories but other people's, and they fill your head with darkness. You realise you're on your knees, looking up into the blank eyes of your opponent.

"Goodbye, Seagrave. Your memories will be most useful to us."

He smiles as his sabre puts an end to your quest.

169

Thinking quickly, you show the card the butler gave you.

"You must not have seen me, I'm here on business."

She apologises and steps aside to let you pass.

Turn to **33**.

170

You flip the coin over and she tucks it away inside her tattered coat with a nod. Deduct 1 SHILLING.

Turn to **343**.

171

"Ladies and gentlemen, allow me to introduce Private Seagrave."

Eldritch circles you, her heels loud and hollow on the wooden stage.

"Formerly Sergeant Seagrave until sentenced to death for conspiracy against The Order."

She sweeps the umbrella over her head in a black arc until the tip comes to rest against your neck. The guards grip your arms tightly and force you to your knees. She smiles and presses the cold tip into your throat, making you gasp for air.

"And now Private Seagrave returns to the scene of the crime. To see a fellow-conspirator make the ultimate sacrifice for The Order. For which we give thanks."

She bows her head briefly and the crowd does likewise. Her eyes gleam cold and dark in the dawn light.

"But what do you say, my friends – shall we make this a day to be doubly grateful? Shall we sacrifice Seagrave as well?"

She spins on the spot and spreads her arms wide. The crowd roars its approval as you cough and gasp and take a deep, rasping breath.

She bends down and whispers sweetly into your ear.

"I thought they might say that."

A second block is brought out and the guards force your neck onto a groove worn smooth by use. You look over at the Watcher. She hasn't moved this whole time. The blindfold is still in place, but why is she so still? So quiet? The executioner steps forwards and Eldritch nods. All is ready. The faces in the crowd are hardened by misery, lined by fear, and their eyes follow the executioner's axe hungrily as it rises high above the Watcher's neck.

You cry out. Desperation gives you strength and you half-rise against the weight of the guards pressing you down. And then you hear Eldritch's voice inside your head.

"I won't have this disorder, Seagrave. Do you hear me?"

Her laugh echoes through your mind.

"Of course you do. Now tell me, do you remember what it's like to dream?"

Turn to **7**.

172

Three guards descend the steps, one behind the other. Pulling back your sleeve, you load a bolt and take aim at the one in front...

Roll one DICE. If you roll a...

... 6: you kill him. Fill in both halves of his crossbones below.

... 4 or 5: you wound him. Fill in one half of his crossbones.

... 1, 2 or 3: you miss.

If your SKILL level is 5 or higher, add 1 to each roll. For example, a 3 becomes a 4.

When both halves of his crossbones are filled in, the attacker is dead. After each roll, scribble out one of your twelve bolts below.

FIRST GUARD   SECOND GUARD

If you kill the first two guards before running out of bolts, turn to **346**.

If you run out of bolts before they've both been killed, turn to **181**.

173

The crowd are turning against you. You're going to need proof! And suddenly you notice the way Orson's standing. With his left foot forward slightly, angled outwards. There's something not quite natural about it. You push him aside and get down on your hands and knees.

"Oi!" shouts Orson. "What do you think you're doing?"

He tries to pull you away, but you shout in triumph.

"There! Found it!"

Ignoring Orson's frantic protests, you rip a hole in the green fabric covering the stage. Underneath is a small pedal connected by string to the spinner. Orson makes a noise in his throat, halfway between a laugh and a gulp.

"Oh, that little thing? That's just an emergency brake in case... Wait, you don't think I'd use it to... No, I run an honest game. I..."

His voice rises to a yelp as he realises he's surrounded. But before they drag him from the stage, you search his pockets.

Add all the SHILLINGS you've spent on the game, plus 5 more to your LOG BOOK. Now turn to **53**.

174

You know these streets well, but tonight they feel strange. A nightwatchman calls the hour, and you hear a distant cry. But it's not just the sleepwalkers. There's something else, too. Something you can't put your finger on. Meg climbs up onto your shoulder and her damp fur is warm against your neck. You look at the stars and stop. There's the Summer Cross, just above the roofline. And suddenly you realise why that guard didn't recognise you. Why you're not shivering in your wet clothes. Because it's no longer winter in Mirewick – it's summer! You've been gone half a year.

You take a deep breath. This must be the moment the dragon was talking about. But why? You see a noticeboard and hurry across.

One of the flyers catches your eye – a public execution on the Field of Healing at dawn. And Eldritch will be there! You rip off the flyer. Have you missed it?

"Ah, I like a good execution, myself."

The voice is calm and smooth. You spin around.

"Of course, I generally conduct mine without an audience."

The man is well-dressed in a blue tailcoat and cream waistcoat. He raises his hat and nods courteously.

"Jonas Merton, at your service."

The name rings a bell.

"You may have read something by me. Just trifles, really. Cheap thrillers for the masses."

He takes off his coat, lays it neatly aside and rolls up his sleeves.

"But lately I've taken a more hands-on approach to my research. Aids the authenticity, you know. And passes the nights when sleep eludes me... as it often does, these days."

With a flourish he twists the head of his ivory cane to reveal a wicked barb at the tip.

"Shall we begin?"

JONAS MERTON

Rounds: 5   Damage: 2

YOU

Unknown to you, the barb is coated in poison. If Jonas wins three rounds in a row, deduct the damage and go straight to the defeat entry.

If you win, turn to **113**.

If you lose, turn to **229**.

175

You feint to your right, and as the guard tries to slash down his sabre scrapes against the stone wall. You grab his arm and twist it around until the weapon drops from his grasp. A blow to the back of the head buckles his knees, and you drag his limp body into the shadows.

Turn to **79**.

176

You sense you need to lighten the mood.

"From one person of good taste to another," you say, indicating her hat.

She laughs and runs a hand over the feather.

"You haven't done much haggling before, have you dearie?"

She pauses, then extends a leathery hand.

"Three shillings."

If you want to pay, deduct 3 SHILLINGS and add the CLOAK to your LOG BOOK.

Now turn to **198**.

177

There's a pink glow in the sky and the towers of the Citadel loom over the rooftops. The streets are busy now and your eyes dart left and right, seeing danger at every turn. But there it is, finally. Gateway open and people already making their way through for the execution. The size of the crowd makes you hang back. Surely some of them will be those men in top hats? You take the mirror from your coat pocket and turn it on the crowd, pretending to examine a troublesome tooth. And that's how you see the real Citadel for the first time. The walls are smooth and dark, with a strange, green tinge, and its towers rise like living stone, jaws open to the dawn sky. Above the central tower you see the last ghostly images of the pale river swirling downwards, as if through a plughole.

Your mouth has gone dry. You close it and swallow hard, suddenly aware that you can't hold the mirror up too long. Tearing your eyes away from the Citadel, you search the crowd.

Turn the page to see the view through the mirror. Find all the creatures disguised as men in top hats, so you can avoid them on the way to the entrance. Look for their hollow eye socket, metal teeth and sabre claws. Count them all up and multiply the number by ten, then turn to that entry. And remember that **if you were rolling two DICE after every entry, you no longer need to**.

If you can't find all of them, turn to **342**.

He runs down a dark lane and crouches behind a sign outside a shop.

"Get down!" he hisses.

Gain 1 ABILITY point.

You crouch down behind him and peer out. People have appeared on the square. Dozens of them. Some wander slowly, aimlessly, and others stand still, staring straight ahead.

"What are they doing?" you ask.

Before he can answer, you hear singing and someone stumbles onto the square. As the people turn towards him, the singing stops. The man tries to back away, but the nearest person leaps and drags him to the ground. More of them pile on, but somehow he manages to fight free, his shirt ripped to the waist. He spins around wild-eyed before tearing down a side street. You wait for the others to give chase, but it's strange – now he's out of sight, they seem to have forgotten all about him.

Turn to **10**.

179

"He's cheating!" you cry. "He must be!"

The crowd shifts uneasily.

"You lost fair and square!" someone shouts.

"No!" you cry. "I can't have lost twice in a row – think about it!"

"No, *you* think about it," says a gruff voice by your side.

Suddenly, several pairs of hands are hoisting you into the air.

They throw you off the stage and into the mud.

Deduct 1 ABILITY point.

As you scramble up the crowd steps back. You realise you have your hand on the hilt of your night-sabre. Orson looks down from the stage, with a smirk on his face.

If you decide to wipe that smirk from his face, turn to **133**.

If you decide to leave, turn to **53**.

180

You return his gaze.

"I'm here to show everyone who Eldritch really is," you say. "I'm here to break her precious Order."

He nods and smiles grimly.

"What's the plan?"

You tell him you need to get close enough to use the mirror, and he offers to come with you, but you shake your head. There's no point risking you both. He puts a hand on your shoulder.

"Listen, I'll speak to my guards, the ones I can trust. If you give the sign, we'll be ready."

You grasp his arm. The two of you were cadets together. Old comrades.

"I've seen enough without that mirror..." he says, tailing off. Then he smiles sadly. "And I'm not getting much sleep myself these days. Don't think it will be long before those men in top hats are coming for me."

You see the dark circles around his eyes and realise the truth of what he's saying. He steps across to the door.

"You'd better hurry," he says. "They'll be starting soon."

You nod your thanks and turn back onto the passageway. The crowd is thinner now, and there's a gateway up ahead. This is the entrance to the Field of Healing – a large courtyard in the heart of the Citadel. You walk through into the cool dawn air. A dark tower looms above, and on the far side is the stage, where the executioner stands by his block, head bowed under a grey hood. The crowd chatters excitedly, but a hush descends as a tall, thin figure emerges onto the stage. Eldritch. She's wearing a black dress and a black top hat, and she speaks with a ringing voice.

"Today we are gathered to celebrate the dawn of a new day. A day that's free from the terrors of the night."

She pauses and points with her umbrella.

"Free from the one they call the Watcher."

The crowd cheers as a young woman is brought on. She's wearing a blindfold, but her clothes look two hundred years out of date, and the noise around you seems to fade as you see who it is. Mary Finch. The girl from the painting.

Roll one DICE and add your SKILL level.

If your total is 10 or higher, turn to **57**.

If it's 9 or lower, turn to **289**.

181

You rip the crossbow from your wrist, but before you can draw your night-sabre the guard strikes. You stumble back one step, two... and into the canal. Clawing your way to the surface, you see the woman casting off, calling something. And you realise you never even knew her name. Not that it matters now, with the dark waters reaching down your throat. Your adventure is over.

182

Standing at the top of a steep slope, you see the tracks below where the train will slow. You scramble down into a thicket of brown bracken and peer through the stalks. The wait is a long one and Meg buries herself inside your coat to keep warm. Not many trains travel north beyond Mirewick. But finally you hear the toot of a locomotive's whistle, and here it comes, wheels squealing as it takes the bend. The carriages pass, not as slowly as you were expecting, and you burst from cover as the last one goes by.

Roll one DICE and add your ATHLETICISM level.

If your total is 9 or higher, turn to **323**.

If it's 8 or lower, turn to **114**.

183

Lifting the cloak, you stumble and put your hand down on something warm and soft. There's a bark and a jabbing pain, and a dog's head emerges. It must have been asleep! Deduct 1 LIFE point.

The cart stops and the old lady appears around the back.

"You'll get your breakfast soon, Milo!" she shouts.

Then she sees the teeth marks and blood on your hand and her eyes narrow.

"A thief!" she shouts. "A stinking thief! And a guard too!"

"Look at his hand," she says to the people that have gathered.

"Caught red-handed!" one of them cries.

"Never mind that," she says, not willing to let the mood lighten. "He tried to pinch that woollen cloak, didn't he? It's worth five shillings if it's worth a penny!"

Your eyes goggle. Five shillings!

The crowd closes in.

"Think carefully," one of them growls.

If you decide to pay, turn to **337**.

If you decline, turn to **119**.

184

You peer through a small window and see a luggage room, dimly lit. There's no one in sight. You reach for the handle, but the door is locked.

If you have a ROLL OF TOOLS, turn to **261**.

If not, turn to **297**.

185

Your breath comes in ragged gasps. You feel your strength failing.

"Seagrave!" Blake shouts. "Stay with me!"

His hair is matted with sweat and blood. His uniform is torn to shreds, yet somehow he's still standing. For a brief moment your eyes meet, and too late you realise his plan. With a great roar he launches himself at Eldritch, meeting her claws with his chest. He's lifted bodily into the air, and in that brief moment, her side is undefended. You step in and run your sabre deep. To the hilt.

This time there's no scream. You stumble back, and a strange feeling washes over you, a kind of awakening, a clearing of the mists. Your sabre clatters to the stage and suddenly you realise there's nothing left *to* scream. Eldritch is gone. Down below, the guards are rubbing their eyes and blinking in the fresh dawn light. The men in top hats have gone too. You hear a familiar voice inside your head. Eldritch. Weak and far away.

"They won't remember a thing, you know. You saved them all, and they've already forgotten."

Her laughter fades.

"Until next time, Seagrave…"

You hear a soft sigh by your feet. Blake lies on the stage, two holes in his chest where the claws had been. You kneel down and cradle his head in your arms.

"We did it, Seagrave," he murmurs. "We did it…"

A look of confusion clouds his face.

"We did… what?"

As his eyes close, you lean close.

"We saved them. Just remember that."

You're not sure how long you kneel there with your head bowed, but slowly you feel something soft and wet nuzzling your hand. It takes a moment to realise – it's Meg. Her fur a little singed, but the same old glint in her eyes. You cry out with relief and go to stroke her, but she gives you a sharp nip, then taps the mirror with her hooked tail.

"You're right, Meg," you say. "We'd better get that back to Skerramore."

Turn to **242**.

186

Making your way up the ravine, you tread carefully over the icy rocks. Down here the ground is in shadow and everything is still. But suddenly, something zips past your ear and buries itself in the snow. You whirl around, and the second missile strikes you hard in the chest. Deduct 1 LIFE point. As you dive for cover, you glimpse a strange creature drawing its head back into a hole in the cliff. It has red, saggy cheeks and a long, vulture-like neck. The wind whistles by as you crouch behind the boulder. Slowly, you peer over the top, but the creature emerges, cheeks bulging like two red balloons. You duck, and the missile shatters on the rockface behind. It's made of bone. The monster must be eating its prey whole and then using the bones to catch its next meal...

If you have the MINIATURE CROSSBOW and want to use it, turn to **381**.

If not, turn to **291**.

187

The organ music plays and the pictures of the ring toss game move from side to side – each one a memory from your adventures. But which one to choose? The dots and dashes on the ticker tape are some kind of code, but when you look at the puppet by the machine, he just stares back with blank, painted eyes. And then you notice another line of dots and dashes, this one running around the frame of the bar. You lean closer. There's an 'A' on the left side and a 'Z' on the right. And the dots and dashes are split into sections. One for each letter of the alphabet? You count around. The first letter would be 'S', the next 'K'... After decoding everything on the tape you get 'SKERRA'. Skerramore, surely! You've already seen it, there on the top row. The barman gives you a ring and you toss it over the key. He pulls it from the lock and holds it out.

"I hope you enjoyed your stay at The Last Gasp," he says.

As you take the key, the organ music stops and the dummies collapse to the floor.

Add 1 ABILITY point, then turn to **154**.

188

You step down, shoulder to shoulder with Ada and her gang. Suddenly, one of them drops to the floor.

"Get out of my head!" he cries.

You flinch as you feel something inside your own head. A pressure, a probing, something looking for a way in.

"Attaaack!"

Ada raises her night-sabre high and you all charge.

If you still have the PENDANT, turn to **304**.

If you no longer have the PENDANT, turn to **86**.

189

You walk up and tap the glass hatch separating the driver's cab from the carriage. Without turning round, the driver waves you away. You tap again. Harder. He turns and you point to the latch. Shaking his head, he mouths something you can't quite catch above the roar of the engine. As the tram slows for the station, you shatter the glass with your elbow. There are cries from the carriage as you bring the tip of your night-sabre level with the hole.

"Ladies and gentlemen," you shout. "We won't be calling at the next stop. But please stay calm," (you look the driver in the eye) "and normal service will resume."

The tram picks up speed again. The guards at the station hold up their hands and step into its path. Your instincts were right! The driver waves his arms frantically and they jump clear just in time. The station flashes past. Gain 1 ABILITY point.

Wheels screech as the tram hurtles around the bend, ash and steam rushing into the carriage. You think quickly. They'll be sending a signal down the line. Grabbing the driver by the shoulder, you tell him to ease up. You look out of the doorway and wait for the right moment to jump...

Roll one DICE.

If you roll an even number, turn to **324**.

If you roll an odd number, turn to **251**.

190

You can't delay any longer. Aiming by sight, you release the trigger. The whole boat rocks as the ballista fires. You jump aside to avoid the recoil, so Ada is the first to see – and your heart sinks as you hear her cry:

"You missed! You missed!"

Deduct one ABILITY point, then roll one DICE.

If you roll 1-2, turn to **82**.

If you roll 3-6, turn to **207**.

191

The toad sails high through the air, too high, and lands harmlessly beyond the stage. You missed. Turning around, you see a town guard just a few paces away. His eyes widen in recognition.

"There he is!" he shouts, pushing a prisoner aside and drawing his sabre.

GUARD

Rounds: 5   Damage: 1

YOU

If you win, turn to **283**.

If you lose, turn to **62**.

192

Your ankle jars as you plunge deep into the snow. Cold and limping, you struggle out of the drift and see Demon's Well rising above you. As the airship turns towards home, you begin your climb.

Deduct 2 LIFE points, then turn to **137**.

193

Something hard hits you over the back of the head. Your knees buckle and you feel someone helping you to the floor. Deduct 1 LIFE point.

You wake up with Meg prising your eyelids open. Blearily you get to your feet. The monster has gone, and so have the sleepwalkers and men in top hats. You walk down to the riverbanks, rubbing the back of your head, and see the shore has been churned by many feet. Suppressing a shudder, you hurry back the way you came.

Turn to **174**.

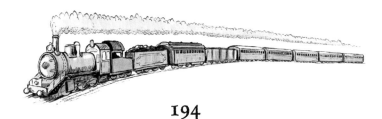

194

On the far side of the courtyard there's a passageway leading deeper into the Doldrums. Bare clotheslines stretch between the windows and the sky is just a strip of grey. Suddenly you notice a small creature hanging from one of the lines. It's a fisher, swinging gently from the hook on the end of its tail, green eyes almost glowing in the gloom. They've come from foreign lands, these creatures, but they've learnt to thrive in the dark alleyways of Mirewick. And you see there are more on other lines, on window ledges – you've never seen so many in one place before. Normally they only fish for cats or rats, but now they follow you in silence. The end of the passage still seems a mile away when something brushes the top of your head. You look up and see green eyes barely an inch from your own.

Time to run!

Roll one DICE and add your SKILL level.

If your total is 8 or higher, turn to **227**.

If it's 7 or lower, turn to **125**.

195

"He's cheating!" you cry. "I saw it slow down!"

"What are you talking about?" someone calls from the crowd. "Course it slowed down!"

Roll one DICE and add your SKILL level.

If your total is 8 or higher, turn to **173**.

If it's 7 or lower, turn to **284**.

196

The fury and weight of his strokes forces you back, and your heel catches on a loose cobble. He raises the shovel high, and it hangs for a moment, grey against the dawn sky. Then he brings it down and all goes dark.

197

Past the aqueduct are the western reaches of Mirewick. The canal runs alongside a crumbling wall overhung by old trees. Ada slows the boat.

"This is where you get off, Seagrave. Pendle Rise is beyond the wall."

But she tenses as a tall man in a top hat appears around the bend.

"Get down," she mutters.

A few moments later she taps on the hold, and you come back up.

"Can't be too careful," she says.

You nod and grasp her hands. She smiles.

"Go on. I'll get as far away as I can before leaving the boat." She pats the roof. "Sorry, old girl, but you've got the guards after you now."

"So have you," you say quietly.

"Don't you worry about me."

She gives you a push towards the shore and you step off.

"Oh, wait!"

She rummages in her pockets and tosses you something small and dark. It's a pendant of dark stone hanging from a cord.

"My good luck charm," she calls. "I found it floating in the canal one day. I don't know – there's something about it. But I think you might need it more than me."

Add the PENDANT to your LOG BOOK, then turn to **221**.

198

Up ahead, the mill looms through the rain, ten floors high. As the crowd nears the iron gates it grows quiet, and that's when you hear the sirens of the Citadel, announcing your escape. How long have they been wailing? You nearly freeze on the spot, but force yourself to keep moving. The crowd flows between the gates, and beyond them the road is almost clear. Almost. You look again and see four guards advancing towards you. Has someone seen you?

If you have the CLOAK, turn to **247**.

If you don't, turn to **281**.

199

The organ music plays and the pictures of the ring toss game move from side to side. But no matter how hard you stare at them or the ticker tape message, you can't work out which one to choose. The puppets watch you in silence, with their blank, painted eyes, and the barman holds out a ring.

"Why not try your luck?" he says.

You take the ring and throw it over one of the keys. The organ stops, the lamps go out, and in the darkness you hear the dummies dropping to the floor. Eldritch laughs softly.

"The game's over, Seagrave."

You feel a slight tickle on the back of your neck, and then you drop to the floor too.

200

Suddenly you feel Meg bursting from your coat. She leaps back into the cave and there's a huge roar as you scrabble clear of the entrance. The dark river rushes beneath, and you grab hold of a tree root to stop yourself slipping down the icy slope. You're only just in time. The bear bursts into the open, Meg's hook buried in its bloodied nose. There's a moment when you think it will stop, dig in with its mighty claws. Its small, hard eyes meet yours, but then it's gone, tumbling down with a bellow of rage. Far below there's a splash, and the fast-flowing waters sweep the beast away.

"Meg!"

Your cry echoes down the valley.

"Meg!"

You haul yourself back onto the path and lean over the edge, but you see no sign of the tiny creature that just saved your life. The cold wind sighs in the branches above, and slowly you turn to go. There she is. Sitting a bit further along, cleaning the hook on the end of her tail as if it were all in a day's work! And your cries of relief are muffled by the soft snow.

Turn to **356**.

201

There are many routes to Pendle Rise, but two that seem best.

If you'd like to make your way through a rich area filled with big townhouses, turn to **316**.

If you'd like to cut through the grounds of Mirewick's largest prison, turn to **39**.

202

His silence unnerves you, and you begin to stretch the truth. You tell him how the girl pointed out the owl symbol, and said you could find help wherever you saw it. But your voice sounds thin and unconvincing.

"We got on very well," you finish tamely.

He strokes the dog's head.

"I think she was having you on, whoever she was. I've not seen the owl, but it's probably just graffiti."

He turns a card over and places it carefully on the table.

"Like I said, I'm just waiting for an early delivery. That's why the door was unlocked. My dad lives in the rooms above. If you come back at lunchtime, you can talk to him. That's when we open."

If you want to threaten him, turn to **150**.

If you'd prefer to offer him a bribe, turn to **4**.

If you decide to climb back up to the courtyard, turn to **249**.

203

They fight like they're trying to wake from a nightmare – wild, desperate, flailing arms and legs. But the whole time their eyes are glazed and dull. In the morning they'll have no memory of this. You spin your sabre around and use the hilt to send them properly to sleep. They'll have sore heads tomorrow, but there's no other way.

A blow to the back of the head knocks the last one down, but when you look up there are more sleepwalkers drifting onto the square. Dozens of them! You freeze on the spot, your chest heaving. But suddenly you hear snatches of a song, and a man comes stumbling over the cobbles. He sees the sleepwalkers too late and tries to back away, but the nearest two leap and drag him to the ground. You hadn't thought they could move so fast! Somehow, he manages to get to his feet, shirt ripped to the waist. He spins around, wild-eyed, and tears down a side street.

The whole thing lasts no more than a minute, but in that time, you see the guard watching from the shadows of a dark lane and run across to join him.

Turn to **10**.

204

The lock gives way even more easily than you were expecting, and the door flies open and knocks over a pile of luggage. Stepping quickly inside, you wedge the door shut with a large suitcase. You're about to go through into the next carriage when a red-suited attendant opens the door.

"I thought I heard a noise," she says, looking at you suspiciously. "I didn't see you walking past."

If your SKILL level is 5 or higher, turn to **169**.

If it's 4 or lower, turn to **377**.

205

One of the guards falls, the shovel wedged deep in his shoulder. He cries out in pain, but you see your chance and the cook grunts as the hilt of your sabre connects with his head. His eyes meet yours and suddenly he looks lost.

"Where am I?" he mutters, as he topples like a felled oak.

The other guard runs over to his companion and kneels down. He puts his head to his chest and stays there for a long moment. Then he closes the guard's eyes and looks over.

"I know you, don't I? You're Seagrave."

You stay silent, and he seems on the verge of saying something else, but then he gives a short laugh and looks back down at his friend.

"Good luck to you," he says softly.

You nod your thanks and look at the fallen bodies around you. Anger wells up inside, and as you turn towards the Citadel you swear vengeance against Mayor Eldritch and her Order.

Gain 1 ABILITY point, then turn to **122**.

206

He nods to himself, and you see something you hadn't noticed before, beneath the swagger. Rage.

"You see these hands, officer?"

He holds them up.

"They were too light for you just now, but I reckon they'll be too heavy for you too."

And with a wink to the crowd, he attacks before you have time to draw your sabre.

Turn to **101**.

207

You jump back behind the bow and see the guards' carriage shake as their ballista fires. You wait for the impact, but it never comes. They missed!

"The smoke!" Ada yells. "Look at the smoke from the train."

It's going straight up in the air.

"And look at the chimneys!"

Then you see it. The smoke from the chimneys is being blown by the wind, but the smoke from the funnel isn't. The train must be moving the same speed and direction as the wind! You glance at the wind speed dial and adjust your aim... and this time there's no mistake.

"A hit!" Ada cries. "A direct hit!"

Turn to **366**.

208

The toad sails through the air in a long, croaking arc, and just as Edmund draws his sabre, it slaps him in the face. His hand goes to his cheek and the crowd holds its breath.

"This will not stand..." he stutters. "This cannot stand..."

"So sit down!" someone shouts, lobbing a boot that strikes him in the belly and draws an indignant 'ooof!'

"You see how they wrong me?" he cries, turning to his fellow actor on stage. "Will you stand by?"

And just as the prison guards move to quell the disturbance, he launches himself into the crowd. More actors follow, running out from behind the stage, and the prisoners surge to meet them. The town guards are swept forwards in the melee, shouting and holding on to their hats. Your plan couldn't have worked any better. In the confusion you slip away and run the short distance to the woods.

Turn to **44**.

209

You climb into the hammock and Meg curls up on your chest. But the temperature in the cabin steadily drops, and the cold seeps into your bones. The moon shines through a porthole, filling the cabin with a pale white light, and as you drift off to sleep it feels like an eye in the dark, glimmering with malice.

Add 2 LIFE points, then turn to **124**.

210

Something tells you that silence will serve you best here. His breathing slows and you feel his hold relaxing. He sighs and seems to lose interest.

"What do I care if they kill you? You've killed enough of us."

He wipes his mouth and steps away.

"I want two shillings for my troubles."

Your eyebrows rise at the price.

If you'd like to pay him, turn to **64**.

If you decide not to, turn to **293**.

211

You lower the looking glass and turn around. Suddenly you remember the words that echoed through the chamber.

"What curse?" you shout. "What do you mean?"

The dragon looks at you with ice-blue eyes.

"I mean, Seagrave, that something isn't right. Don't you feel it? Lying in the dark when sleep won't come. Maybe you're afraid to sleep, afraid to wake from another dreamless night. But do you ever wonder why that is?"

It bends down, a white flame flickering from its jaws.

"Why don't you dream, Seagrave?"

"I-I don't know," you stutter. "Maybe I'm dreaming now."

The chamber shakes with the dragon's laughter.

"If only you were."

You wait for the echoes to subside.

"Who are you?"

"I am the First Watcher. And I was a man once, a long time ago. But that is not important. Our time is short."

The voice is getting fainter, and you realise the dragon is fading.

"Listen closely, Seagrave. If you can't dream, then you can't see the world as it really is. So let the mirror show you. Take it back to Mirewick. Find Eldritch. Because she's the one that takes them, Seagrave. She came for your dreams... They all did."

If you want to ask who 'they' are, turn to **127**.

If you want to ask if it means the invaders, turn to **54**.

212

You hear distant sounds from the corridor behind – at any moment your escape could be discovered. But which door is the way out? One more time you lean over the rail and peer down. But the harder

you try to retrace your route, the more you get muddled. Deduct
1 ABILITY point.

You're just about to have a guess when a door opens below. A
guard walks in rubbing his head, and through the open doorway you
see a low-hanging lamp. You remember hitting your head on the
same thing! Or at least, there's a good chance it was the same. The
guard closes the door and walks on. Now's your chance. Your
footsteps echo as you make your way down, and taking a deep
breath, you open the door. Just off to the side is a spiral staircase –
the way you came in!

Turn to **326**.

213

You turn to the butler and shake your head.

"I don't know what to do," you say. "Have I failed?"

He looks around the room.

"You are failing, but you have not yet failed. I can't help you..."
He pauses for a moment, and his mouth twitches. "But perhaps
there are three others in the room that can. Which painting are they
all pointing to, Seagrave?"

Deduct 1 ABILITY point, then turn back to the picture on **294**.

214

He holds your gaze steadily. This is a man who risked his neck to save yours, but you find it hard to trust anyone after what you've seen.

If you want to tell him the truth, that you're here to confront Eldritch, turn to **180**.

If you decide to lie and say you're here to beg Eldritch's forgiveness, turn to **134**.

215

A group of guards walk down the steps, one behind the other. They'll have to fight you one at a time, so you must defeat the first guard before attacking the second.

FIRST GUARD

Rounds: 5   Damage: 1

SECOND GUARD

Rounds: 4   Damage: 1

YOU

If you defeat the two guards, turn to **144**.

If you don't, turn to **306**.

216

You flatten yourself against the wall, the explosion still ringing in your ears, and when you turn around it's as if you're dreaming. Because there's a dragon, glistening like ice, with its tail curled around the column. Its long neck curves down to the looking glass and its voice echoes through the cavern.

"*A mirror made from the breath of the First,*
Held to the light shows the source of the curse."

The dragon roars and white flame curls from its jaws. Something starts to form within the frame of the looking glass, and you find yourself walking jerkily forwards. It's as if your legs aren't your own. Taking a deep breath, you grasp the handle and lift it towards the light.

Look at the picture opposite. If you follow the dragon's instructions correctly, a number will be revealed.

If you can't find the number, turn to **55**.

217

"Come now, we can't let this stand," Orson says, laying a hand on your shoulder. "You name the stake. Whatever you want, and I'll double it if you win. One last opportunity to come out ahead. This time you only need to spin a two or above."

Decide how many shillings you want to stake and delete that amount from your LOG BOOK. Then roll one DICE.

If you roll 2-6, turn to **123**.

If you roll a 1, turn to **5**.

218

You stand on the edge of the precipice, hesitating, searching desperately for a safe way down. Deduct 1 ABILITY point.

"Seagrave!"

The Watcher has almost disappeared down into Eldritch's throat, and still you hold on as Skerramore comes apart piece by piece, until the floor you're standing on gives way and you tumble into the void, spinning down and down and into the Watcher's outstretched hands. The moment before you touch she grins in relief – and then there's a flash.

Turn to **389**.

* Fold the top page down to see how Seagrave's outstretched hands meet the Watcher's.

219

You slump to the floor in front of the gates. Above you, the wrought iron lettering of 'Mirewick Prison' stands out against the sky. And then the letters lose their focus, and you fall face down on the ground. Your adventure is over.

220

You step to the side, but his great sledgehammer of a fist still catches you a glancing blow that sends you staggering back. Your hand flies to your night-sabre, and you stare at each other for a few moments – then he turns and lumbers off into the crowd.

Deduct 1 LIFE point, then turn to **198**.

You follow the red-brick wall around to the gates, but the old gatehouse is empty. Beyond, the driveway winds up through wooded parkland. You find a section of wall that's covered with ivy and start to climb. The vine thickens as you get higher, and you reach deep to grab the rough, twisted branches near the wall. Wiry tendrils cling to your arms and smother your face, but finally your groping hand clasps the top and you haul yourself over. On the other side, trees rustle softly overhead. The city suddenly seems very far away. The old house sits on top of the hill, and you set off through the parkland, picking your way over damp, mossy ground. There's a flash of something white, a deer bounding away through the trees, and behind are the grey stones of the house. The woods reach almost to the walls. You find a pair of wooden doors with a great metal handle and knock three times. Silence. You look up at the dark windows, the great, lichen-covered stones. The house seems to be holding its breath. And then you hear a bolt being drawn back, and a latch lifted. The door creaks open.

"Can I help you?"

The voice is clear and precise. A butler steps into the light, his uniform immaculate, his grey hair combed neatly to one side above wire-rimmed spectacles. You realise you're at a loss for words. *Can he help you?* What are you expecting, exactly? You see the absurdity of your vague, half-formed hopes and feel the panic rising in your chest. What if he were to turn you away? A polite but firm apology ushering you into the arms of the guards. He clears his throat and you blurt out the first thing that comes to mind.

"She's dead. Malory. That was her name. She whispered

something to me. Skerramore."

His eyes flicker to your uniform.

"No, no," you stutter. "It's not, I'm not... They're the ones trying to kill me!"

If your SIXTH SENSE level is 5 or above, turn to **160**.

If it's 4 or below, turn to **75**.

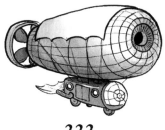

222

The situation is hard to read: the guards could just be performing routine checks, or it could be something more sinister.

If you'd like to carry on to the ticket office, turn to **340**.

If you decide to turn around and try hopping on the train further down the line, turn to **182**.

Or if you'd prefer to charter an airship instead, turn to **34**.

223

You give them a brief rundown, leaving out the slightly embarrassing detail about giving away an item to avoid any trouble. When you've finished, you ask to be let through to make your report to the warden. The second guard looks at the first, who nods reluctantly, and they open the gates to let you pass.

Gain 1 ABILITY point, then turn to **76**.

224

"Is two shillings the going rate, then?" you ask.

Slowly, the boy puts the deck of cards into his top pocket and holds out his hand.

Deduct 2 SHILLINGS, then turn to **158**.

225

You run back along the walkway and there's a sudden rushing sound as the water gets sucked down and explodes upwards. Water and ice rain down, and you dive forwards to avoid a large chunk that shatters on the walkway.

Turn to **216**.

226

She winces and shakes her head sadly.

"It's not your day, is it?"

She totters towards you, pretending to use the cane like a walking stick. Then suddenly she stops dead, twirls it high into the sky and catches it mid-pirouette.

"I'm Evie Nightshade, and I'm afraid I'm going to have to kill you. Don't be angry."

She leaps forwards.

EVIE NIGHTSHADE

Rounds: 6   Damage: 1

YOU

If you win, turn to **328**.

If you lose, turn to **56**.

227

A fisher lands on your neck, but you fling it off before it can bite. Slithering over the wet cobbles, you dash towards the end of the passageway. You feel them on your back, around your feet, their sharp teeth tearing at the coarse material of your guard's coat. But somehow you keep your balance and emerge onto a wide square unscathed.

Turn to **43**.

228

You walk back past the stall where the old man was sitting with his dog. The covers are down and you hear a whine from inside. Through a gap in the canvas you see him sitting. His face is pale and clammy, and his hands grip his thighs, knuckles white. The big dog lies cringing on the floor and standing over them both is a man in a top hat. You watch for a moment, but neither man says a word. The silence is eerie.

Then you hear the chatter of voices and turn to see where they're coming from. Someone lifts the flap of a large, white tent, and you see tables and benches inside.

What was that smell? Soup? Stew, even? The cook stands behind a steaming pot, his dirty apron straining against a huge belly underneath. You pause. It's getting on for mid-morning now, and you haven't eaten since last night.

If you'd like to go in, turn to **116**.

If you decide to carry on for Pendle Rise, turn to **201**.

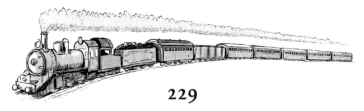

229

You feel the poison from Jonas's cane making its way through your veins. Finally, you sag to the cobbles. Meg whines and licks your cheek, and as the world goes dark, you hear Jonas whispering to himself.

"A guard with a fisher for a pet. What a delightful embellishment!"

230

The bottle smashes against the wall too far away from the fisher, and the creature screeches but doesn't drop its catch. Instead, it climbs up and over the wall, dragging the cat with it. You brush a shard of glass from your shoulder and turn back onto the lane.

Turn to **334**.

231

"Very good, Seagrave. It's almost a shame to see such a capable brain separated from its body."

Gain 1 ABILITY point, then turn to **135**.

232

Amid the roars and screams from below, you fight the guards.

If you lose a round, add together the damage ratings of the two guards, then take the total from your LIFE points. If a guard is dead, don't add their damage rating. If you win a round, deduct the COMBAT points only from the guard you chose to attack. And remember to keep a note of how many rounds you have left for that guard, too.

FIRST GUARD

Rounds: 4   Damage: 1

SECOND GUARD

Rounds: 5   Damage: 1

YOU

If you win, turn to **73**.

If you lose, turn to **258**.

233

You sink to your knees, your vision blurred, one eye swollen shut. Blake's uniform hangs tattered and bloody, yet somehow he's still standing, and with a great roar he throws himself at Eldritch, bringing his sabre down with all the strength he has left. But it's not enough. The creature meets him in mid-air and slams him down. The stage splinters under the weight of the attack and your friend's body lies broken and still at last. You stagger to your feet and charge, all tactics spent, all hope gone, and Eldritch lifts you into the air, impaled on her two long sabre-claws. As your eye slowly shuts, you see the battle taking place all around. The guards driven back, only a few left now. One more goes down, clutching his head, unable to keep the darkness at bay any longer. It's the last thing you see.

234

You trudge on for a few more minutes and reach a point where you can see the railings stretch into the distance. Seeing no obvious weakness, you realise your best bet is to use your information on Evie.

Turn to **375**.

235

She stops and eyes you suspiciously until you ask the price of the cloak.

"Ah, a gentleman of some taste," she smiles, revealing a top row of silver teeth. "And by that I don't just mean you, dearie, I mean the previous owner too."

A cloud passes over her face briefly.

"Three shillings," she says.

You look at her open-mouthed. Three shillings for a tatty cloak!

If you'd like to pay her, turn to **109**.

If you want to try to drive the price down, turn to **52**.

If you'd prefer to walk away, turn to **198**.

236

Orson scratches his chin, as if thinking.

"I tell you what else I'll do, because I don't like to see an honest guard out of pocket, I'll shorten your odds. All you have to do is spin a three or above."

He puffs out his cheeks and shakes his head, as if he can't quite believe what he's saying. The crowd murmurs its approval.

"And let's double the stake. I'll pay double too. That way you'd come out ahead."

After a slight hesitation, you hand over the money and spin the wheel hard.

Deduct 2 SHILLINGS from your LOG BOOK, then roll one DICE.

If you roll 3-6, turn to **322**.

If you roll 1-2, turn to **96**.

237

The man draws his sabre from beneath his long coat.

MAN IN TOP HAT

Rounds: 5   Damage: 2

YOU

If you win, turn to **88**.

If you lose, turn to **168**.

238

You wake as the first rays of light catch the windows of the tower above. The crowd is shouting and pointing. The block next to you is empty – the Watcher has gone. Eldritch raises her hands, her face a mask of fury.

"It's a trick!" she cries. "There's the real traitor."

She sweeps her umbrella down and the executioner moves across. You try to get up, but find your wrists are tied to a ring at the base of the block. Squinting desperately into the sunlight, you follow the eyes in the crowd as the axe rises behind you. And that's when you feel something stir, something hidden inside your coat. It's Meg – she's back! With a fierce chirp, she reaches for the mirror lying forgotten on the stage and holds it up, shielding your eyes, reflecting the sunlight onto Eldritch instead. For a moment the mayor of

Mirewick stands unmoved. Then her head tips back, and you hear that same, inhuman scream. You grit your teeth, and when you look up, she's gone. In her place stands the creature, taller than any man. And her umbrella has changed too, replaced by a staff with a glowing tip. The crowd shrinks back as she points it at Meg. A bolt of lightning flashes across the stage, and you cry out as Meg sinks to the floor with a soft whine.

Then, as if from a great distance, you hear Blake's voice piercing the silence.

"Now! Now is the time!"

The crowd breaks apart and there are the guards, turning on the men in top hats. The spell is broken, and the creatures stand revealed. Blake scrambles onto the stage and cuts your bonds. Together the two of you turn to face Eldritch.

If you have the WHISTLE, turn to **126**.

If not, turn to **278**.

239

"Now don't you think that fingers as light as these deserve some kind of reward?"

He turns to the crowd for support.

"Shall we say a shilling?" he asks.

"Make it two!" someone calls.

The pickpocket shrugs his shoulders and smiles.

"The people have spoken."

If you're willing to pay the money, turn to **64**.

If you're not, turn to **206**.

"It used to be one or two a night," she says grimly. "Now it's *hordes*. And they're dangerous, some of them. They haven't slept for weeks, months. It does something. They end up like this. In some kind of nightmare. Half-asleep, half-awake."

She looks you in the eye.

"But they don't remember a thing when they wake up. That's why we try to save them from those men, from that monster."

If you want to ask another question, turn to **308**.

If you want to get on your way, turn to **365**.

241

She flits through the trees like a will-o'-the-wisp and it's all you can do to keep her in sight.

If your ENDURANCE rating is 6 or higher, turn to **336**.

If it's 5 or lower, turn to **46**.

242

The gates are open, and Arkwright the butler is there to greet you by the door. Meg leaps onto his shoulders, and in her excitement, she knocks his spectacles askew.

"I see you've left your manners on your adventure," he says sternly.

But as she jumps down and scampers inside the house, his eyes glisten and he can't quite hide a smile.

"She knows there's a treat waiting for her in the kitchen," he says, smoothing down his grey hair. "Welcome back to Skerramore."

He holds open the door and leads you through to the great hall, where a table is laid. You see a letter beside your plate.

"From the 27th Watcher," he says. "She asked it be kept for this moment."

He turns to go.

"Arkwright," you say. "What about the sleepwalkers? Will they get better?"

He meets your eye with the hint of a smile.

"I'd say it's nothing a good night's sleep can't fix, Seagrave."

As he goes out to see to your meal, you pick up the letter.

Seagrave, I'm so glad you're reading this. It seems only yesterday that it was me sitting there, reading a letter from the 26th Watcher. I remember how tired I was. How awfully tired. I wonder if he felt the same when he was reading his letter from the 25th! Did he want nothing more than to curl up on the rug by the fire and sleep? Because yours was not a new fight, you know. It is the oldest fight there is. Eldritch will be back. Not next year, maybe not for a hundred years, but she will be back. And when she returns, will you be there to meet her? Will you be the 28th? That is the choice you must make. When we met in the dream-space you received the gift of remembrance. It is a dubious gift, but one easily returned. If you walk away, your memories of Eldritch and her creatures will fade like everyone else's. And if you stay? Well, your picture will go up on the wall. You could be there a long time, but time is a funny thing here on the Other Side. So, that is all. I do not need to tell you the consequences of walking away. You have seen the early stages of it. But you are young, I understand. I chose someone older, but fate intervened.

Enjoy your meal, Seagrave. And take your time – you've earned it. Mary Finch, the 27th.

Putting down the letter, you realise that Arkwright has laid out the food. It smells good, and as you eat, you stare at the portraits above. Meg comes in and sits on the arm of your chair. She smells of marmalade.

"It wouldn't be so hard, Meg, if you could come with me."

You hear someone clear his throat behind you.

"And if she could come with you, would you stay with us, here at Skerramore?"

You turn around. Arkwright looks at you calmly, but in his hands he's twisting a napkin. You realise what he's offering, even though he would miss Meg very much.

If you choose to stay, turn to **40**.

If you choose to leave, turn to **374**.

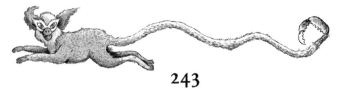

243

"Hold on, Meg."

You make a leap for the grass verge but catch the rail and come down hard on the gravel. Wincing, you look up to see the attendant waving cheerfully from the carriage door. Meg pokes her head out and licks the graze on the side of your face.

Slowly climbing to your feet, you begin the trek back to charter an airship.

Deduct 1 LIFE point, then turn to **34**.

244

The moans are coming from a small chamber just off the main corridor. On the far side, a gas lamp flickers above a metal door.

If your SIXTH SENSE level is 4, turn to **58**.

If it's 3, turn to **140**.

245

Using the hook as a foothold you swing your legs over, but your foot slips and you grasp the railings to stop yourself falling headfirst. There's a burning pain in your thigh, and after you've lowered yourself to the ground, you see a nasty gash. Cursing under your breath, you repack the rope and set off through the grounds.

Deduct 1 LIFE point, then turn to **76**.

246

You run down to the embankment and send the bottle spinning and arcing over the water. It disappears into the monster's cavernous throat, but the creature doesn't even seem to notice.

"What was that?" Ada calls.

"Sleeping potion," you shout.

She looks at you like your dad used to when you made the wrong move in a game of cards.

"You going to sing it a lullaby?" she says, turning back to face the men in top hats.

Deduct 1 ABILITY point and delete the SLEEPING POTION from your LOG BOOK. Then turn to **188**.

247

You finger the cloak, unsure what to do.

If your SIXTH SENSE level is 4 or higher, turn to **309**.

If it's 3, turn to **353**.

248

Something looms over you, and it takes a moment for your eyes to focus. It's Meg, with her big, green eyes. She chatters excitedly and the butler pushes her off your chest.

"Drink this," he says, handing you a teacup. "It's still hot."

You're slumped in a chair. The seat is deep and you shuffle back and take a sip. You feel the stairs rising above you. The painting must still be up there, but you don't want to look.

"Is she still there?" you ask.

The butler inclines his head.

"She's waiting for you."

"What is she?"

"I think you should address your questions to my lady."

You nod slowly and drain your cup. You haven't come all this way to leave now. Mounting the stairs, question after question races through your mind. You turn to face the painting, and she's not swinging any more. She's waiting for you, just as the butler said.

"All your questions can be answered by one word, Seagrave – magic."

She didn't even let you open your mouth.

"You don't believe in magic, do you? Even in my time the old beliefs were gone. But the magic is still there. I found that out... and you will too."

She looks at you sadly.

"You'll find out more than you want."

Her change of tone catches you off-guard, but after a moment's pause, she carries on.

"Take the looking glass to Demon's Well in the Whistling Mountains. There the mirror can be remade."

"Demon's Well?" you ask warily, and she nods.

"From Mount Scarfell, look due east. Demon's Well is at the tip of the witch's nose."

You wait for her to continue, but she pushes off from the soft grass and starts to swing.

"Is that all?" you say, your voice rising. "Is that all you're going to tell me?"

She leans back.

"No. There is one more thing. You may have heard rumours of an invasion that's coming… Well, they're wrong. Because it already happened. Years ago."

She meets your eye.

"They're already here."

You feel a curious sense of distance opening up between you. Her voice is fading.

"The mirror will show you the one who rules the invaders. I cannot see their face. Their magic is too strong. But Seagrave…"

You lean forwards to catch her words.

"Beware the men in top hats. You must get to Demon's Well – before they get to you."

You open your mouth, a hundred questions on your lips, but Mary Finch, 27th Watcher of Skerramore, is frozen once more, mid-arc.

Turn to **341**.

249

You nod slowly and turn around. Once back in the courtyard, you weigh your options. There are two routes to the Citadel that seem best.

And remember that now you're above ground again, you need to roll two DICE at the end of each entry, following the same instructions as before.

If you'd like to go past the cotton mill, turn to **274**.

If you'd like to cut through the backstreets where the mill workers live, turn to **110**.

The deathly cold of the guard's night-sabre spreads out from your chest and seeps into your bones. Slowly, you sink to the ground. The passengers look down from the carriage as the rain falls on your lifeless body.

251

You jump too soon, slip on the wet cobbles and land hard on your side.

Deduct 1 LIFE point, then turn to **108**.

252

You look around the circle and realise the odds are hopeless. Your shoulders slump and the circle parts.

"It was an evil star that saw your paths cross," the old imp says as you walk away.

You turn.

"Your eyes..."

"Are closed to all the dreamless ones. Perhaps it keeps out the lie."

In silence you retrace your steps.

Turn to **129**.

253

You're driven back under the fury of his onslaught, every blow sending a dull ache shooting up your arm. He backs you up against a wall and swings hard, and as you duck his shovel strikes the wall with a loud clang. Now's your chance. He grunts as the hilt of your sabre strikes his head, and staggers backwards. A look of surprise spreads across his pale, sweaty face.

"Where am I?" he asks, before slumping to the ground.

Breathing hard, you look down at his unconscious body.

"I had no choice, Meg," you mutter.

And as you set off for the Citadel once more, a quiet, cold fury quickens your stride.

Turn to **122**.

254

It's a tricky situation to read. You didn't have much choice – she attacked you, after all, and was clearly dangerous. But at the same time, it could complicate matters – and you haven't got time for complications...

If you decide to tell the truth, turn to **362**.

If you decide to lie, turn to **81**.

255

You don't see the killing blow, coming as it does from a neat sidestep and strike to the back of the neck. As you lie gasping on the cold cobbles, you look up and see Pendle Rise, so close now. What would you have found there, you wonder, as your eyes lose focus and your gasping finally stops.

256

The smell of brimstone fills your nostrils as you strike the final blow.

"Just a pile of rags," you hiss, kicking over the two steaming top hats that stand empty on the ground.

Then, with a deep breath, you turn towards the Citadel.

Turn to **122**.

257

You're left in the empty chamber, with the blue evening sky above and the dark stars below. The clocktower wavers on the water, its hands pointing to four o'clock. Not long before dawn. But the dawn of what day? Meg peers down at the water.

"Are you..."

She jumps before you can finish your sentence. As the ripples spread, you take a deep breath and leap after her. The water punches you in the gut and knocks the breath from your lungs. Invisible hands drag you down, down, until it feels like you're falling, and then your head breaks the surface and you hear the clocktower chiming the hour. You open your eyes and see it rising above you. Meg's face appears level with your own and you clamber out of the water feeling strangely refreshed. The aches and pains you felt a moment ago have vanished.

Restore your LIFE points back to 12.

Looking down, you see a small, black puddle. It's not even deep. However you got here, there's no going back. But suddenly, there's a sound from across the square. Someone is running towards you. A guard! Your hand reaches for your sabre, but he looks over his shoulder and tears past without stopping.

If you'd like to follow him, turn to **178**.

If not, turn to **148**.

258

As you sink to the floor, a great, bloodshot eye peers through the shattered window. Its slit-pupil roves the office and lands on your stricken body. The beast grunts and reaches inside. Slowly, almost delicately, you're lifted into its warm jaws.

259

You press down three keys and noise once more fills the floor. But this time there's a discordant edge to it. Something stretched and grating. The beasts lift their heads and see the workers running for cover, the guards edging away. One of them leans down so its face is level with theirs, back glistening with sweat. It roars, and the window in the office rattles. The manager squeaks in horror.

"Stop it!" he cries. "You don't know what you're doing! They'll tear this place apart!"

You smile grimly and tell him that's the idea. Gain 1 ABILITY point.

One by one the beasts bellow, almost drowning out the notes that goad them on. And suddenly they're on the move – tearing and smashing and hurling and biting. You duck as a guard is flung towards you, his eyes wide with terror. The window smashes and he lands in a heap on the desk.

Then two more guards burst through the door, night-sabres drawn. You look from them to the shattered window. One of the beasts lurches past, and up close you see a chain around its neck. Something to hold on to...

If you'd like to fight the guards, turn to **232**.

If you decide to make a leap for the beast's back, turn to **164**.

260

Stepping past the guard, you open the door to the hollow centre of the tower. It looks more like a deep well from up here, dropping floor after floor into darkness. You peer over the edge and see small figures standing below. To reach the door that you were brought in by, you'll have to be sure and quick – any hesitation will arouse suspicion. But it won't be easy. You weren't a tower guard, and they brought you in blindfolded. Your only hope is to remember the route.

Turn over to see the tower, and use your memories to retrace your steps. You'll be going in the opposite direction this time though, so you'll have to do everything in reverse. When you think you've found the exit, turn to the number on the door.

If you can't find the right door, turn to **212**.

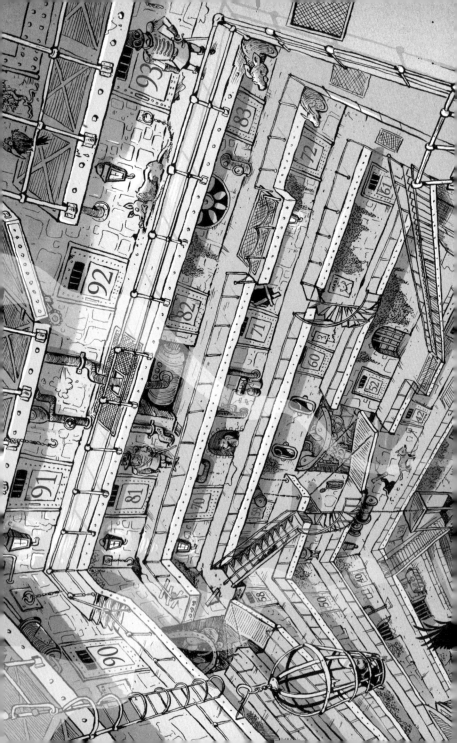

You close your eyes and think back. You remember hearing the cries of the ravens as you entered the hollow core of the tower. The air was cold and damp. You turned left out of the door then almost immediately right. You remember a hand on your shoulder making you wait. Pulleys squealed as a gangway was lowered into place. You walked across, climbed a staircase and turned right at the top. A dog growled as you mounted a spiral staircase. At the top you turned right, and felt a hand on your shoulder once more. A drop of water trickled down your back as you waited. Bolts slid across and a door opened. The door you've just come in through. You open your eyes and look down...

The lock looks a simple affair. Taking a thin screwdriver, you insert it into the keyhole and turn gently. It takes a moment to find the right spot, and then, above the noise of the train, you hear a click. You try the handle again, and the door swings open. Stepping into the carriage, you put the screwdriver back in the roll.

Gain 1 ABILITY point, then turn to **33**.

262

"And why would I do that?" Eldritch sighs.

Deduct 1 ABILITY point.

"None of them will open. You're a guest here until you wake up... Or in your case, until you die. Which won't be long now."

Her voice is light and playful.

"You should thank me, really. Giving you this extra time and some peace and quiet, away from the crowd."

You try another door.

"Who are you?" you ask, as the handle rattles and the door stays shut.

Turn to **333**.

263

His hold gets tighter and tighter until stars burst in your vision, then everything goes dark. When you wake, you're on the wet cobbles and three guards are standing over you.

"Just found him lying here," one of them is saying. "Looks like he got himself in a spot of bother."

"That was silly, wasn't it?" one of the others says, nudging you with his boot.

He sighs.

"We'd best get him back."

This time, your execution goes ahead as planned.

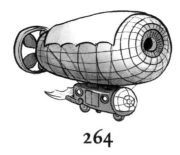

264

You stare out at the ground below, repeating the clue over and over in your head. But you can make nothing of it. Deduct 1 ABILITY point.

Gambrel circles the ship back around and passes over the peak once more. Suddenly, he points to the east.

"Look!" he cries. "That inlet could be a mouth. That lake an eye... And just to the north – that volcano, that's got to be the witch's nose!"

And there it is. You wonder how you didn't see it before – the side of a witch's face on the ground below. You clap Gambrel on the back and laugh. Meg uses the excitement to pinch his pipe and scamper to the rear of the cabin.

"Give me back my pipe!" he roars. "Bleedin' fisher."

Turn to **270**.

You climb into a small cabin filled with sacks and crates.

"Make yerself comfortable," says Gambrel, shifting a few boxes around. "There's a hammock slung across the stern, and plenty of crates to rest yer legs."

He makes his way to the helm up front. Through the open door you see the ship's wheel and various instruments and levers. You sit yourself by a porthole and look back towards the aerodrome, but just as you're settling down, the doors to the terminal open. Two guards step out, accompanied by a tall, thin man in a top hat. He points to the low fence you climbed over. The guards seem to be trying to explain themselves, almost cringing before him, and you remember the Watcher's words. You shout a warning towards Gambrel.

"Don't worry," he calls. "I've seen 'em."

You feel a jolt as the ship is released from the mast, and as you rise above the aerodrome, your beating heart slows. Any later, and that fence would have been under watch. Outside, the propeller splutters into life and the whole of Mirewick spreads out beneath you. Meg climbs out of your coat and leaps straight into the hammock.

"Aha, a stowaway!" Gambrel says, looking behind him. "That'll cost extra."

He brings the ship about. The sun is setting, and over his shoulder you see the dark line of the Whistling Mountains, like ashes beneath a fiery sky.

"I'd get some rest," says Gambrel. "You look like you could use it."

If you have the CLOAK, turn to **302**.

If not, turn to **209**.

266

You pretend not to hear and carry on walking. Halfway across the courtyard a stone strikes you on the back of the head. One of those children has excellent aim. You hear them retreating down the alley behind you but don't give chase. Gingerly, you feel under your hair and see blood on your fingertips.

Deduct 1 LIFE point and turn to **343**.

267

You fumble slightly as you draw your night-sabre and the element of surprise is lost. The two guards step back and unsheathe their weapons.

"I knew it!" the first guard says, and spits to one side.

If you lose a round, add together the damage ratings of the two guards, then take the total from your LIFE points. If a guard is dead, don't add their damage rating. If you win a round, deduct the COMBAT points only from the guard you chose to attack. And remember to keep a note of how many rounds you have left for that guard, too.

FIRST PRISON GUARD

Rounds: 4   Damage: 1

SECOND PRISON GUARD

Rounds: 5   Damage: 1

YOU

If you win, turn to **6**.

If you lose, turn to **219**.

268

With a sure step you light the lamp and edge back along the boat to the cabin.

Turn to **19**.

Firelight flickers through the small windows of the thatched cottage. You knock on the door and a voice replies that's dry and cracked.

"Who's out there, with the snow a-swirling? Come in, come in and warm your toes."

The latch is lifted and a tiny old woman ushers you inside. She's wearing a large red headscarf and a white dress hangs loose over her skinny shoulders.

"Sit, sit," she chides, pushing you weakly towards a rocking chair by the fireplace. Above the flames hangs a big pot of stew. The hearty smell reminds you that you haven't eaten since breakfast. Meg pokes her head out from your coat and sniffs deeply.

"Ah, will you look!" the old woman claps happily. "One more."

She smiles and drops another turnip into the stew.

"Take off your boots," she says. "Stretch out your legs."

She bends down and throws some branches on the fire. They give off a sweet smoke and you breathe deeply. Meg yawns on your lap. You say you weren't expecting to come across anyone living out here, so far from the city, and she smiles again as she stirs.

"Oh, you just never know when something's going to drop in your lap."

You nod sleepily. It certainly was a stroke of luck. You wonder why she doesn't seem interested in what you're doing out here in the forest, but it doesn't really matter. Nothing much does. Anyway, you can hardly remember.

"You have a little rest, dear, while I add the finishing touches to this stew."

You nod slowly and settle your head on the cushion. Through

half-closed eyes, you see her sack in the corner. A heavy sack, you think, for one so old. There's something white inside. What is it? Bones. Your eyes close. Bones...

If you have the PENDANT, turn to **30**.

If not, turn to **118**.

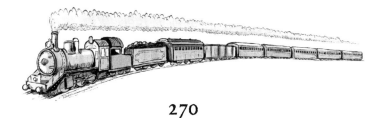

270

Gambrel brings the ship around.

"Let's pick that old witch's nose!" he shouts, launching into a fast and furious shanty about a woman with seaweed for hair.

He stamps his feet to the beat to keep warm, and you watch the mountains pass below, the deep valleys and pine forests, and wonder what you might find at Demon's Well. There's a knot in the pit of your stomach, and you pick up Gambrel's newspaper to distract yourself. '*Eldritch Calms Fears in Sleepwalker Mystery*'. You imagine her jabbing a sleepwalker with her umbrella and smile. She doesn't seem the sort to scare easily.

You're still reading the paper when Gambrel's singing stops. You don't even hear him cursing quietly and wrestling with the wheel. You only notice there's something wrong when he calls you up to the helm.

"SEAGRAVE!"

You see dark clouds to the north, looming like a colossal wave. There's a flash and a crash that judders your bones.

"Can't outrun it," Gambrel roars, as the storm engulfs the ship. "We need to get lower."

Meg burrows down inside your coat, and Gambrel grabs your arm. His voice is fast and urgent.

"I'm going to need help."

He shows you a wheel at the side of the helm.

"Turn clockwise to go up, the other way to go down. Keep as close to the mountains as you can without crashing."

A flash illuminates his face, his eyes wide, and then he leaps back to the ship's wheel as the wind swirls and roars. It's all he can do to keep the ship upright. You peer though the gloom, through the snow spattering the windshield, and wait.

If your SKILL level is 5 or higher, turn to **347**.

If it's 4 or lower, turn to **41**.

271

The trick is to act as if you're doing nothing wrong. You slip a pie into your bag and let out a sigh. The woman glances over and you explain you've left your money at home. You even raise your eyebrows as if to ask whether she'd gift a hungry guard his breakfast. Her small eyes narrow and her chin recedes behind several pink folds. You shrug and walk out of the shop.

Further down the street, you take the pie from your bag and take a bite. The hot gravy runs down your chin and you wipe it away with the back of your hand. As you let Meg steal a bite, you feel some of your strength returning.

Add 4 LIFE points, then turn to **177**.

You look out of the window as the tram pulls in. They're probably just on their way home. But your fists are clenched in your lap. Out of the corner of your eye, you see one guard go to the front entrance, and the other move to the rear. They're not just on their way home! You spring to your feet and run to the back – your only thought is to fight them in the open. The guards start running, but you leap from the tram and turn to face them.

You'll have to fight them both at once. If you lose a round, add together the damage ratings of the two guards, then take the total from your LIFE points. If a guard is dead, don't add their damage rating. If you win a round, deduct the COMBAT points only from the guard you chose to attack. And remember to keep a note of how many rounds you have left for that guard, too.

FIRST GUARD

Rounds: 5   Damage: 1

SECOND GUARD

Rounds: 4   Damage: 1

YOU

If you win, turn to **87**.

If you lose, turn to **250**.

273

The cook wipes the sweat from the red folds of his neck with a damp cloth. Then he ladles your stew into a bowl and pours a mug of strong tea. Deduct 1 SHILLING.

You sit down and spoon the stew into your mouth. It's thin, but hot and peppery, and you feel it warming you inside and out.

Add 5 LIFE points, then turn to **167**.

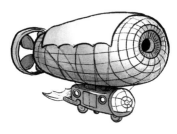

274

The Citadel isn't far, but every noise you hear, every figure you pass makes your heart beat faster. Meg can probably feel it. She pokes her head out and sniffs the air. Up ahead is the mill. It looks different, somehow, and as you get closer you see the outer walls are topped with glass shards and barbed wire. There are sentries on the gates. As you pass, you ask if it's been a quiet night.

"Had worse," the short one calls. "Most of them were over to the west. They got into the prison on the hill."

"The sleepwalkers?"

"Course the sleepwalkers!" He shakes his head. "Best place for 'em."

Further on, you hear a sudden cry. Closer this time. And around the corner you see a large man surrounded by three guards. He has a filthy apron tied over his nightshirt and a shovel in his hands. It's the cook from the market! With a great roar he swings the shovel and knocks one of the guards clean off his feet. The man doesn't get up, and one of his companions sees you and calls for help.

If you'd like to help, turn to **329**.

If not, turn to **72**.

275

Slipping through a gap to your left, you notice a coin on the floor. You stoop to pick it up without breaking stride.

Add 1 SHILLING to your LOG BOOK, then turn to **198**.

276

The attendant smiles and takes your bribe.

"Welcome aboard."

Turn to **33**.

277

You hand over the money and spin the wheel hard.

Deduct 2 SHILLINGS from your LOG BOOK, then roll one DICE.

If you roll 3-6, turn to **322**.

If you roll 1-2, turn to **96**.

278

Eldritch flexes her long sabre-claws. She must be twice the height of you or Blake, but at least there are two of you.

Add your SKILL, ATHLETICISM and ENDURANCE levels.

If your total is 18 or higher, turn to **349**.

If it's 17 or lower, turn to **61**.

279

A big smile spreads across her face, and she claps her hands once.

"Oh *good*," she cries. "This is going to be so much fun!"

She twirls her cane high into the sky and catches it mid-pirouette.

"I'm Evie Nightshade, and I'm so glad we can play."

She leaps forwards.

EVIE NIGHTSHADE

Rounds: 6   Damage: 1

YOU

If you win, turn to **328**.

If you lose, turn to **56**.

The ogre's club whooshes past your ear, smashing down left and right. You scrabble to your feet, sweat glistening on your brow. But finally, you find a way through and your sabre bites deep. The beast howls and drops its club.

"Stop!"

The cry is high and clear. It comes from Ivy. She's being held by two imps, but they let her go and she steps forwards.

"Do you think I'd go with you?"

The painted eyes stare straight at you, and she chuckles.

"Not if you killed twenty ogres. In this place I still have my dreams."

You look at her in confusion, and in the silence she smiles sadly.

"Do you even remember what they are?"

Slowly, you sheathe your sabre. The old imp turns and asks darkly: "Why did you come here, Dreamless One?"

Turn to **36**.

281

You can't risk walking past the guards, and turning against the flow of the crowd would arouse suspicion. Your only option is to follow the workers though the gates to the mill.

Turn to **372**.

282

Your resistance is weakening. With a last, desperate attack, you force your opponent back. He stumbles against one of the sleepwalkers and they drag him to the ground. The cold tendrils slip from your mind as you run him through.

Gain 1 ABILITY point, then turn to **142**.

283

As you drive your opponent back, the prisoner who was shoved aside leaps on the other town guard. You hear roars from the crowd, but it's not until your opponent lies still on the grass that you take in the turmoil you've unleashed. The prison guards are fighting to restore order and the actors have long since left the stage. You see the other town guard slumped face first on the ground, and quietly slip away, running the short distance to the woods.

Turn to **44**.

284

You feel the crowd turning against you. In desperation you grab Orson by his shiny red waistcoat and give him a shake.

"Tell them!" you say through gritted teeth. "Tell them how you cheated."

Orson winks with the eye the crowd can't see.

"Trade secrets, I'm afraid," he murmurs under his breath. "Watch out!"

You feel heavy hands on your shoulders. Suddenly you're lifted into the air and thrown offstage into the mud. As you scramble up the crowd steps back. You realise you have your hand on the hilt of your night-sabre. Orson looks down from the stage, with a smirk on his face.

If you decide to wipe that smirk off his face, turn to **133**.

If you choose to leave, turn to **53**.

285

Not knowing why, you grasp the pendant around your neck. The one that Ada gave you. The effect is instantaneous. The man draws back as if struck and an image flares in your mind. But this time it's not a memory, not something you've seen. It's Mirewick in flames, people in chains, and someone looking down over all, someone you can't quite see. Then it's gone. And *he's* gone. The man. His top hat sits on a crumpled overcoat, and you slump back, panting heavily. Where did he go?

Without realising it, Ada gave you a pendant that protects its wearer from dark magic. But you see its power is limited. The attack has left the stone tarnished and dulled – it will only be able to save you from one more black magic attack.

Turn to **388**.

286

Self-consciously, you smooth the coat of your uniform. You see the wariness in his eyes and remember how the girl looked at you the same way. He's not going to believe she told a guard about their secret symbol. So you tell him the truth, how you noticed the carving of the owl on the doorway. How you asked her about it, but she didn't respond. How you need to get to the Citadel, but you're on the run, no longer a guard. He turns over a card from the deck and places it on the table slowly.

"Why'd you want to go back to the Citadel, anyway?" he asks.

If you want to tell him about the mirror and what it shows, turn to **387**.

If you decide to keep that to yourself, turn to **313**.

287

You open the pouch and find five shillings inside. There doesn't seem to be anyone in the crowd searching for it. You run your thumb over the leather. It's an expensive-looking pouch – whoever dropped it probably won't miss it anyway. Pocketing the money, you press on towards the fair.

Add 5 SHILLINGS to your LOG BOOK, then turn to **12**.

288

The guard backs you into a corner. You feint and lunge, but he's too fast and his sabre bites deep. A cold emptiness spreads through your veins and you sink to the floor. From far above, you hear the inmate shouting something crazy about an invasion. About monsters. Not that it matters to you, as your eyes close for the last time.

289

There'll be more of those men in top hats here, you know that. But you haven't a moment to lose – and it's too crowded to use the mirror yet anyway. So trusting to luck and a little judgement, you start to weave your way through. On the stage you see the Watcher down on her knees. How did Eldritch find her? How is she even here? You remember the skeletal hand that passed you the mirror and your head spins. But you've taken your eyes off the crowd in front, and as people jockey for a better view, you bump into an old lady with a pinched face. She draws up her shoulders and looks down her nose.

"Do you mind?" she says. "Guards in my day had better manners."

Her voice attracts the attention of others nearby, and you see two tall top hats slowly turning. The hair beneath is lank and grey, and the faces are pale. Their lips draw back in a bloodless snarl and you feel a sudden, numbing pressure. From all around the creatures attack, flooding your mind with black despair. Deduct 2 LIFE points.

And then there's a voice inside your head, cold and amused.

"Leave this one be. I want them up on stage."

As you're pushed towards the front, the pressure recedes. This is your chance. You fumble for the mirror and angle it towards her.

"Look!" you shout desperately. "Look at what she really is!"

There's a moment's silence, and then people start to laugh.

"Why don't you look yourself?" someone calls.

And you do, and she looks the same, there in the glass. No hollow eye, no sabre-claws. Just an amused and victorious smile as you're hauled up onto the stage.

Turn to **171**.

290

"She did nothing wrong!" you shout, drawing your sabre.

The imps remove the ogre's blindfold and let go of the ropes. Its small, red eyes blink in the firelight, and then settle on you. With a deep growl the beast raises its club.

OGRE

Rounds: 5   Damage: 1

YOU

If you win, turn to **280**.

If you lose, turn to **351**.

291

You crouch with your back against the boulder. The monster's got you pinned down. Closing your eyes, you try to think clearly. Your only weapon is your night-sabre, but you can't get close enough to use it. You rack your brains as Meg pokes her head from your coat. Absentmindedly you go to stroke her, and she sinks her teeth into your finger. As you suck the blood, she chatters angrily. A fisher will never be a pet – you should know that. You've seen them use old umbrellas to skewer rats before. Skewer rats… Suddenly you look down, and Meg meets your eyes as if she knows what you're thinking. You draw your sabre and she grasps the handle with her hooked tail.

"It'll be dangerous," you whisper. "But I can distract it. Buy you some time."

She twitches her nose impatiently, and you nod. Leaping up, you watch the monster emerge. The head looks like some kind of troll, its huge red cheeks already bulging. The long neck is covered in white, blood-stained fur, and you can't even guess what lies behind that. Its black eyes are fixed on you, but that's what you want. As the first missile leaves its mouth, you see Meg out of the corner of your eye, creeping across the ravine.

Roll one DICE and subtract it from your ATHLETICISM level. The result is the number of LIFE points you lose as you attempt to dodge the creature's assault. Update your LOG BOOK.

The urge to duck is almost overwhelming, but then you see Meg standing on the cliff-top above. She whirls your sabre over her head, swinging it down in a smooth, black arc. There's a cry, cut off, and a thud as the monster's head hits the floor. Breathing deeply, you lean back against the boulder. Meg scampers down the long, limp neck, and you crouch down to greet her.

"Wait till I tell the butler. He'll make you the biggest sandwich you've ever seen!"

The two of you carry on up the ravine. There's a steep scramble beside a fast-flowing stream, and then your path slips back into the forest.

Turn to **356**.

292

The cave is too small to fight in – and the bear too big. Your only chance is to escape. But where's the entrance? As the bear's eyes blink slowly open you run your hands along the walls, frantically looking for the hole. It would be covered by branches and leaves, but all you find is cold, hard soil. There's a low, dangerous growl, and you spin around to see the bear rise up. Through its legs is a glimmer of light, and you realise that if you want to get out alive, you'll have to get past the bear...

Roll one DICE and add your ATHLETICISM level.

If your total is 9 or higher, turn to **325**.

If it's 8 or lower, turn to **163**.

293

You clear your throat and tell him no. As your hand moves to the hilt of your night-sabre, the crowd start to jeer. The man draws himself up, playing to the crowd.

"I was a good worker," he says. "Straight as a die. But now I can't sleep, and my mind starts to wander."

He turns and walks back to the tavern with slow, dignified steps.

"I just hope the same thing never happens to you."

Someone flips a coin his way, and he catches it deftly. Red-faced, you leave the scene as quickly as possible.

Deduct 1 ABILITY point, then turn to **162**.

"I must apologise," the butler says. "Meg can be a little overzealous in her duties."

He steps neatly aside and holds back the door.

"Please come in."

You hesitate on the threshold.

"A fisher?" you say, and he nods.

"I rescued Meg from some children who'd tied a firecracker to her tail. They mistook her for vermin, but I assure you she's very clean – and clever."

You step inside and see her sitting on a rafter, cleaning the hook at the end of her tail. Beneath her, light slants across a faded tapestry on the wall.

The butler's footsteps ring out on the flagstones, and you follow him down a long corridor. Finally, he stops at the entrance to a grand hall and turns to look at you coolly. His words come fast and precise.

"The lady of the house welcomes visitors who are welcomed by the house. By this I mean that you will not find her unless the house itself allows."

He pushes his spectacles back up onto the bridge of his nose and waits.

You ask what he means, but he holds up a hand.

"Please step into the hall. If the house judges you worthy, it will point the way."

Turn over to see the hall. Look carefully, and if you see where the house is directing your attention to, turn to the number you find.

If you're at a loss, or guess incorrectly, turn to **106**.

The organ music plays on as the pictures of the ring toss game move from side to side – each one a memory from your adventures. But which one to choose? The dots and dashes on the ticker tape are clearly some kind of code... The puppets watch in silence with their blank, painted eyes, and Eldritch starts to laugh softly. You don't know how to break it. But you remember there was another time that someone sent you a dream-like message. It was in the fortune teller's tent, and she gave you those cards... Suddenly they're in your hand! You place them down on the bar, face up – one, two, three. The lamps flare and one of the keys starts to twitch. The one in the picture of Skerramore. It falls to the floor and the barman picks it up.

"Some might call that cheating," he says, handing it over.

Suddenly the organ music stops, and the dummies collapse to the floor.

Turn to **154**.

296

As you walk across a small boy sees you and hisses to the others. They form a silent, defensive circle in the rain. Pushing them aside, you see a bundle of dark fur on the ground. It's not moving.

"It was only a fisher," an older girl says, eyeing your Guard's badge. She puts her hand on the young boy's shoulder. Turning the creature over with your boot, you see the small body and big green eyes; the long tail with the single, hooked claw at the end.

"It fished up Jordan's cat and bit her."

"So we got him with a stone!" the boy shouts.

Fishers came from a foreign land, but have adapted well to the streets of Mirewick – especially the poor areas with high buildings and low light. You look up, and see one sitting high on a window ledge. Its hook scrapes the ledge below.

Turning away, you set off across the courtyard.

"Spare a shilling for the poor?" the girl calls.

If you want to give the children 1 shilling, turn to **170**.

If you decide to give them 2 shillings, turn to **60**.

If you don't want to give them anything, turn to **266**.

297

The lock looks old and weak – it shouldn't be difficult to force. Resting your back against the guard rail, you kick the door.

Roll one DICE.

If you roll 1-2, turn to **204**.

If you roll 3-6, turn to **84**.

298

You land in a deep drift and climb out, cold but unhurt. Demon's Well rises above you, and as the airship turns towards home, you begin your climb.

Turn to **137**.

You're about to head back to the gates when something shifts in the corner of your eye – in the trees beyond the fence. You crouch behind a bush and wait. Yes, there's someone moving towards you, dressed in a prison uniform. His legs are long and spindly, and he picks his way across the ground like a stork, back bent forwards so much that you're not sure how his top hat stays upright on his head. He reaches the railings and looks around before throwing a rope ladder over. You wait for him to climb down the other side before stepping out from behind the bush. He shows no surprise.

"You want to use my ladder."

You stare and ask him how he knows. He smiles slightly.

"You didn't stop me climbing over."

He steps aside. "Hurry please, I need to stash the ladder for later use."

"For later?" you ask.

"Yes, I shall be coming back as usual." He looks towards the city. "Unless I find her."

As you put your foot on the ladder, you ask who he's looking for.

"Mayor Eldritch. I have a single hour before I'll be missed, so I must ask you to hurry."

You climb up and over.

"She can help you?" you ask. "To clear your name?"

He pulls the ladder down and hides it under a bush.

"No. She can't help me. But I have a little present for her. Something to remind her of an old friend."

His eyes are empty and his face is blank. You watch him stalk away on spindly legs, and suddenly a glint from the path catches your eye. You reach through the railings to pick it up. It's a whistle, cold and dark, with a gold rune carved in the side.

Add the WHISTLE to your LOG BOOK, then turn to **76**.

300

You climb up on stage and spin the wheel. The red and blue segments blur into a purple disc and then separate out again. The pointer at the top flicks from one segment to the next, slower and slower.

Delete 1 SHILLING from your LOG BOOK, then roll one DICE.

If you roll 1-3, turn to **28**.

If you roll 4-6, turn to **371**.

301

Your defences crumble under the combined assault of the two men in top hats. Memories swirl in front of you, some your own, some not, until you're no longer sure who or where you are. Weren't you supposed to be doing something? Going somewhere? But why bother? Why not just lie here and let the darkness come? Yes... yes... it's better this way.

302

Wrapping up in your cloak, you climb into the hammock and are lulled to sleep by the deep drone of the engines.

Add 5 LIFE points, then turn to **124**.

303

Poking your head slowly outside, you see she was telling the truth. At the end of the passageway you join the crowds and make your way out through the park gates. They lead onto a cobbled street lined with glittering shopfronts. This is the Jewellery Quarter, where young, well-dressed couples mingle with married men and wealthy widows. You see a tall man in a top hat bend down and enter a shop. He stands out because he doesn't look the sort that would normally buy jewellery, and a moment later the shopkeeper locks the door and pulls the lace curtains across the window. His face is white.

Hurrying on, you glimpse Pendle Rise through a gap in the buildings. It's a low hill that used to be separate from Mirewick itself, but now the city surrounds its ancient walls. You pick up speed with your goal in sight, and almost knock over two guards as you turn into a quiet lane! It takes a moment for you all to gather your wits and reach for your sabres.

If you lose a round, add together the damage ratings of the two guards, then take the total from your LIFE points. If a guard is dead, don't add their damage rating. If you win a round, deduct the COMBAT points only from the guard you chose to attack. And remember to keep a note of how many rounds you have left for that guard, too.

FIRST GUARD

Rounds: 5   Damage: 1

SECOND GUARD

Rounds: 4   Damage: 1

YOU

If you win, turn to **91**.

If you lose, turn to **255**.

304

You feel the tendrils getting a grip of your mind, and your movements slow as the man in the top hat lunges forwards. But there's a flash and a surge of heat from the pendant around your neck. The hat lands at your feet and the man is gone! Only his steaming clothes remain, stretched out as if there were still a body inside.

Make a note of the number of this entry (304).

Then, if this is the first time the pendant's been used, turn to **155**.

If it's the second time, turn to **314**.

Then, turn to **142**.

305

You follow the long curve of the corridor. Gas lamps cast weak pools of light and your pace slows as you near the entrance to the tower. You remember there was a guard post by the door – your only hope is to take it by surprise. Cautiously, you peer around the bend. The guard sits slumped in his seat, chin on chest. His hand dangles by his side and under it lies a bottle. Creeping forwards, you see his stomach rising and falling. He's fast asleep. By the chair you find a guard's uniform, a belt and a night-sabre. There's also a travel bag with a purse full of coins inside. You look back down the corridor. Someone clearly wants you to escape...

As you're changing into the uniform, the bottle catches your eye. It's still half-full, and you haven't had any water since the afternoon.

Add the NIGHT-SABRE (if you don't have one) and 12 SHILLINGS to your LOG BOOK.

Then, if you'd like to take a swig from the bottle, turn to **361**.

If you decide not to, turn to **146**.

306

The force of the guard's attack breaks through your defences. You gasp in shock and stumble back one, two steps… into the canal. Clawing your way to the surface, you see the woman is casting off, calling something. You never even knew her name – not that it matters now, as the dark waters reach down your throat. They fish your body from the canal the next day.

307

It's the rage that turns the tide. Not just your own, but the guard's too. Perhaps they probed his memories, looking for a weakness. But they awoke something inside him.

"Stay away from her!" he roars. "Stay away!"

Each roar is accompanied by a blow from his sabre as he drives his opponent back, heedless of the blood running down his neck, welling out from his side. It's like fighting beside two men, and together you cut the men in top hats down. The guard sinks to his knees as the smell of brimstone drifts away on the morning breeze.

"Where did they go?" he asks.

But in the weak lamplight you can see his eyes losing their focus, closing.

"I don't know," you say, kneeling down next to him. "But I'm going to send the rest of them to the same place, I swear it."

You get to your feet and turn towards the Citadel.

Gain 1 ABILITY point, then turn to **122**.

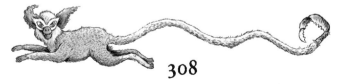

308

If you want to ask about the sleepwalkers, turn to **240**.

If you want to ask about the river monster, turn to **29**.

If you want to ask about the men in top hats, turn to **151**.

If you want to get on your way, turn to **365**.

309

Something tells you that attempting to walk past the guards in a dark cloak will arouse suspicion. And so would turning against the flow of the crowd. Your only option is to follow the workers through the gates.

Turn to **372**.

310

You move up close to the cart and glance around to check no one's watching.

Roll one DICE and add your SKILL level.

If your total is 7 or higher, turn to **14**.

If it's 6 or lower, turn to **183**.

311

The crowd parts as you step down from the stage. They almost seem embarrassed for you.

Add 1 SHILLING to your LOG BOOK, then turn to **53**.

312

No matter which way you turn, somebody always seems to be blocking your path. It's not long before you're out of breath and out of patience. You try to shove someone out of the way without looking, and only realise your mistake when they barely move. It's like trying to push a standing stone. Slowly, the man turns around. His eyes are small and red, and his great fists are clenched.

"Yes?" he says, in a voice that seems to come from some cavernous place underground.

You try to back away, but there are too many people behind. You point to your guard's badge, and that seems to make up his mind. He takes a swing.

Roll one DICE and add your ATHLETICISM level.

If your total is 7 or higher, turn to **23**.

If it's 6 or lower, turn to **220**.

313

You open your mouth, desperate to share the secret with somebody else. But suddenly you realise how it will sound, an ex-guard bursting into the cellar raving about magic mirrors and monsters. He wouldn't want anything to do with you.

"I have my reasons," you say.

He nods slowly and puts the deck of cards in his top pocket.

Gain 1 ABILITY point, then turn to **158**.

314

The pendant glows bright then crumbles to dust in your hand. It won't be able to help you again.

Delete the PENDANT from your LOG BOOK, then turn to the end of the **previous entry**.

315

You wake to the gentle clatter of the train's wheels on the tracks. Stretching your legs, you realise with a start that the man in the top hat is sitting directly opposite! You turn to the window to hide your discomfort. It's dark outside, with stars twinkling above the low light from the carriage. In the reflection, you see the man staring at you.

"The Bottomless Marshes," he says, pointing through the window. "They said we could never do it, you know, build a line over them – but we did."

His voice is calm and detached.

You ask if he works for the railways and he laughs.

"No... but we're all in this together, aren't we? Dreaming a better world."

He smiles, revealing yellow, pointed teeth. The train rocks and

Meg burrows down deeper in your coat.

"But I happened to overhear something you said in your sleep, and it interested me greatly. I thought perhaps I'd misheard, but you said it more than once."

He runs the tip of his tongue across his top lip.

"Demon's Well."

Your breath catches in your throat.

"Yes, that's right. How did you hear of it? We've been searching for a very long time."

He holds your gaze with green, snake-like eyes. Your mouth goes dry, and you tell him you don't know what he's talking about.

"That's a shame. I do have ways of making you talk, you know, but I'd rather not use them."

Your hand flies to your night-sabre but stops in mid-air, as if gripped by an invisible force.

"Very well," he says. "We'll do it your way."

Suddenly you feel a pressure inside your head. A presence. Probing and prodding and peeling back your defences. Memories flicker through your mind's eye and you realise he's searching through them, looking for one in particular – your meeting with the Watcher.

Images flash past like someone rooting through a filing cabinet. Faster and faster, with no order to what you see. Some things long since forgotten... And then you feel a sharp pain in your chest. Meg's tiny claws digging into your skin. For a moment the images fade.

If you have the PENDANT, turn to **285**.

If you don't, turn to **156**.

316

In north Mirewick, the dividing line between rich and poor is the railway line. Cutting through the backstreets, you come to a picket fence that runs alongside the rails. A bottle explodes by your feet and you look around to see laughing young faces in an upstairs window. Further down, a few fence planks have been kicked in. You duck through and hear music drifting across the tracks. There's a row of trees on the far side, and slipping through, you find yourself on a leafy street lined by grand townhouses. A cat watches you from the top of a short flight of steps and licks its paw. Its fur is brilliant white, and the door behind glossy green.

You hear the music more clearly now. It sounds like a fairground organ, and as you set off in the direction of Pendle Rise, the notes get louder, piping up and down, round and round like a carousel. The street arcs down a gentle slope and you see a fair below, nestled among the trees of a small park.

Your path lies through the park, and as you make your way through the crowd your foot brushes a discarded plate of eel pie. Underneath is a small leather pouch.

If you'd like to pick it up, turn to **287**.

If you choose not to, turn to **12**.

317

You pass cell after cell, not really sure what you're looking for, perhaps unwilling to accept the life of a fugitive. If only you could explain that you've no idea why the word was important, the one the prisoner whispered. And you had no intention of finding out.

But that's not how The Order works. No – the word dies with you. Your face stares back from a burnished metal door and you realise you've stopped walking. Carrying on this way is a death sentence. Who let you out? There must be an ally out there somewhere.

You turn back just as a guard rounds the corner. Without stopping to think, you launch yourself towards him – to take him down before he can alert others. He reaches for his night-sabre, but the odds aren't entirely against you. The corridor is narrow and you were trained as an elite guard, skilled in hand-to-hand combat.

Because you don't have a weapon, you must subtract 1 from each dice roll. For example, if you roll for 7 or more to do 1 damage, you must roll 8 or more to be successful.

GUARD

Rounds: 6   Damage: 1

YOU

If you win, turn to **32**.

If you lose, turn to **386**.

318

You see the anger in Blake's eyes. The rage at what's being done in the name of The Order. This is a man you can trust.

Turn to **180**.

319

Blindly you reach for the banister, but your fingers clasp thin air. The stairs tilt sideways and send you tumbling. You hit the bottom hard, and the room goes dark.

Deduct 1 LIFE point, then turn to **248**.

320

You wipe your sweaty palms against your coat. Is it odd to feel so nervous about stealing a pie, after all you've been through? You reach out quickly, but the sudden movement catches the woman's attention. She looks over and her beady eyes narrow. The chance has gone. You walk up to the counter and make a show of surprise when you can't find your money. Her chin recedes into the folds of her neck, and she holds out her hand for the pie. You leave the shop red-faced and empty-handed.

However, all is not lost. Further down the street you feel something warm and wet against your chest. Is that gravy you can smell? You unbutton your coat and find Meg munching on fresh Hangman's Hogget. How she got hold of it you've no idea, but she does at least offer you what's left.

Add 2 LIFE points, then turn to **177**.

321

You slip through a gap to your right and see a small roll of tools on the ground. It must belong to a clockmaker or somesuch. You look around, but whoever lost it is unlikely to find it again in this crowd.

If you'd like to pick it up, add the ROLL OF TOOLS to your LOG BOOK. Then turn to **198**.

322

You grin, sure that the spinner's going to land on a winning number this time. But then it starts to slow quickly, and comes to a halt on the two. Orson bows his head as if he doesn't quite know where to look.

If you want to accuse him of cheating, turn to **195**.

If you want to play again, turn to **217**.

If you'd like to leave, turn to **53**.

323

Measuring your stride to the wooden sleepers of the track, you close on the rear carriage and time your leap to land squarely on the back step. You made it.

Turn to **184**.

324

You time it right and roll smoothly to your feet.

Turn to **108**.

325

The bear yawns and licks its fangs. It takes a step forwards. And another. You smell its warm, putrid breath. Then it swipes, and you duck underneath and dive while it's off-balance. Scrambling up on the far side, you tear at the branches across the entrance, and feel a raking pain down the back of your thigh.

Deduct 2 LIFE points, then turn to **200**.

326

Down and down you run, your shadow stretching before you. There's a guardhouse at the bottom, and you slow to a creep as you draw near. Perhaps this guard will be drugged too... But he's not. He's standing by the gate, looking straight up.

"You took your time," he says.

You don't move.

"Blake?"

He waves you down impatiently.

"It was you – the key?"

"*Come on!*"

You walk down to meet him.

"But they'll kill you if they find out!"

"No reason why they should," he replies, hiding his agitation by unbolting the side gate in the citadel wall. He pauses suddenly and turns. You came through training together.

"You did nothing wrong," he says. "I heard what happened with that prisoner, Malory. Her just whispering something in your ear."

In the distance, a cock crows.

"Now *go*."

He lets you through and bolts the gate before you have time to thank him. Taking a deep breath, you look up. The sky's turning grey and soon there'll be guards out combing the streets. You're a fugitive now, so what would a fugitive do? *Skerramore.* The word rings unbidden inside your head. But as you stare out across the dark city, it makes sense. You lied when the interrogator asked what Malory had whispered. Because it felt like something you shouldn't know. Something they didn't know, perhaps, about that ancient hall – or else why would she whisper? It sits on Pendle Rise a morning's walk from the Citadel, and right now, it feels like your only hope. With a last look back, you set off down the hill.

A cold mist hangs in the air, and as you hurry round a bend, you see a woman standing by a water pump. It squeaks as she pumps the arm up and down, but the bucket at her feet is overflowing, and her dress is soaked. You realise it's just her nightdress, with a shawl over the top. There's a blank, lost look in her eyes, and when you tell her the bucket is full, she doesn't seem to hear. It's like she's half-asleep. You try again, then shrug and carry on down the road.

If you want to catch the early tram, turn to **94**.

If you'd rather go on foot, turn to **17**.

327

Cold tendrils creep down your veins, slowing your movements, filling your head with darkness. You realise you're on your knees, and look up into the blank eyes of your opponent. He grins as he finishes you off.

328

She gasps as your night-sabre slices through her cane and into her arm. The grinning mask drops, and fear enters her eyes.

"Oh!" she says, stumbling backwards. "That's cold."

You take a step forward.

"Evie..."

You want to know why she attacked you. Why she looks like she does. But she looks at you in confusion.

"Evie? Who's that?"

She turns from side to side and passes a hand over her eyes.

"I'm so tired..."

She lies down on the floor, lays her head in her hands, and starts to cry. Sheathing your sabre, you help her into a doorway and leave the lane.

Turn to **335**.

329

Your old loyalties as a guard take over and you rush across. They don't remember who you are, after all. The giant cook blinks, his eyes bloodshot, and swings the shovel like a fly swatter.

SLEEPWALKER COOK

Rounds: 4   Damage: 2

YOU

If you win, turn to **205**.

If you lose, turn to **74**.

330

You're swung from side to side like a rag doll as the beast twists and turns through the streets. People and buildings pass in a blur, and you do well to hold on as long as you do. But finally your grip loosens and the chain slips from your grasp. You hit the cobbles hard. When you look up, the beast has disappeared. From the state of the buildings, you realise you're in a poor part of town called the Doldrums. If there's one place you can hide from the guards, it's here.

Deduct 1 LIFE point, then turn to **162**.

331

With a piercing screech, the last shreeker falls to earth. Gain 1 ABILITY point.

You feel the turret rising, and Gambrel is there to meet you, unbuckling the straps and slapping you on the back.

"Never seen 'em this far south," he says, shaking his head and offering his flask. "I don't like it."

He walks back up to the helm.

"Listen, Seagrave. I don't want any more surprises. We'll reach the foothills of the Whistling Mountains by noon, weather permitting. What's the course?"

You look at the line of mountains up ahead and decide to come clean.

"Mount Scarfell," you say. "But that's not the destination... Or I don't think it is."

You tell him what the Watcher said, and in the silence that follows, his face slowly reddens.

"You've come all this way, risked MY life, for a line from a fairy tale?"

His voice gets steadily louder, and he's about to continue when Meg's tail descends and hooks the pipe from his pocket. He cries out, grabs it, and stuffs it back in his jacket. You try to apologise as Meg chatters angrily from your shoulder, and he stares at you both before finally shaking his head.

"Never should have taken this job," he mutters.

But he turns back to the wheel and you realise you're safe. Quietly, you take a seat by a porthole and watch the shadow of the airship glide over the ground below. Mile after mile of featureless marshland. Then, slowly the marshes give way to stunted groves and rocky outcrops, and around noon, you reach the foothills of the Whispering Mountains. Gambrel points to a snow-covered peak.

"There she is," he says. "The mountain, not the witch."

You see straight away there's nowhere to land, and ask him to fly over slowly, close to the top.

'From Mount Scarfell, look due east. Demon's Well is at the tip of the witch's nose,' you mutter.

Turn over to see the view below. If you follow the clues directly, a location will reveal itself. Count how many squares in from the left it is, and how many up from the bottom. Put the two numbers together to find its coordinates, and turn to that entry.

If you can't find the location, turn to **264**.

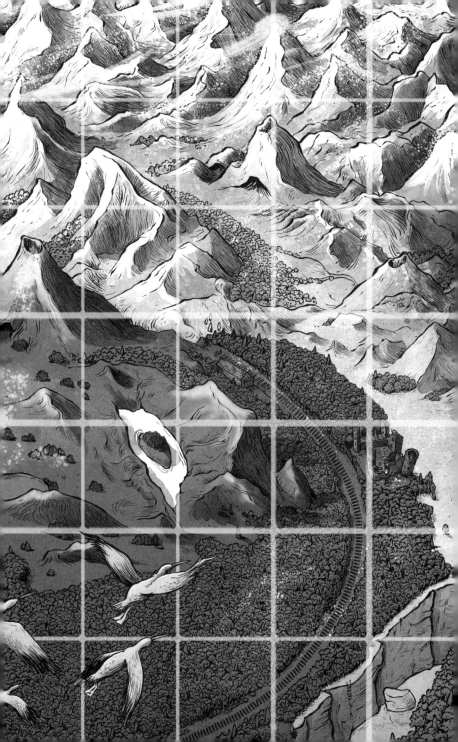

332

You crouch down and run your fingers over the owl. She never replied, that girl in the dark courtyard, when you asked if it marked a secret passage. Maybe there's a whole network of them... You grasp the cold iron ring. There's only one way to find out. The cellar door swings upwards to reveal stone steps and a ramp. Gain 2 ABILITY points.

A lamp glimmers as you descend, and there's a cellar at the bottom filled with barrels and bottles.

"What do you want?"

A boy with brown eyes and a steady gaze looks up from his game of cards. You hear a deep, low growl and see a guard dog beneath the table. You say you're looking for safe passage to the Citadel.

"Then what have you come down here for?" he says. "This is a cellar for the inn. I'm waiting for a delivery."

You tell him you met a girl near the market and gave her two shillings, and she took you through a secret passage past Fisher Street. He doesn't reply, and you weigh up what to say next.

Remember that as you're underground, you don't need to roll two DICE at the end of each entry.

Turn to **9**.

333

"Who?" Her voice lowers. "We are The Order of the Waking Dream. We live off your dreams and die without them. That is all."

You run down the corridor, trying doors at random. Trying not to think about your exposed neck on the block. The axe poised above.

"But have you seen it, Seagrave?"

You pause. She sounds almost wistful.

"The pale river in the sky. Do you know what it is?"

If you want to say it's people's dreams, turn to **231**.

If you choose to say nothing, turn to **135**.

334

Glancing over your shoulder to check you're not being followed, you hurry around the corner and come out on a large square.

Turn to **43**.

335

The streets widen as you reach the edge of the Doldrums. You turn onto a long, tree-lined drive that leads to the prison gates. There are two guards standing watch. The building itself is set in acres of parkland, and ringed off from the world by high, iron railings. You weigh up your options.

If you have a GRAPPLING HOOK and would like to use it, turn to **152**.

If not, turn to **67**.

336

The imp's feet hardly seem to touch the snow, but doggedly you give chase through the dark wood. And suddenly you see a light ahead. A campfire. You burst into the clearing and find her panting in front of an old, white-haired imp wearing a crown of holly. The fire casts deep shadows on her wrinkled face, and you see more imps emerging from the trees, closing around you. Like the one you chased, their eyes are shut, and their eyelids painted. Only the children have theirs open. The old imp raises her hands, and they stand still.

"Did she see you, Dreamless One?"

Her voice is strong, and in the silence she asks again.

"Did she see you with her true eyes?"

The imp you chased tries to speak, but the old one knocks her on the head with her walking stick.

If you want to tell the truth, turn to **100**.

If you decide to lie, turn to **147**.

337

One by one, you place the coins in the lady's leathery hand. It's daylight robbery, but you can hardly complain.

Deduct 5 SHILLINGS and add the CLOAK to your LOG BOOK.

Then turn to **198**.

338

The dog growls even as the hilt of your sabre comes down on its head, and it's only when its legs give way that a soft whine escapes its lips. You step over the unconscious body and search the cellar. The boy has disappeared, and you can find no exit other than one that leads up into the bar. Maybe he was telling the truth after all.

You climb back up to the courtyard and weigh your options. There are two routes to the Citadel that seem best. And remember that now you're above ground again, you need to roll two DICE at the end of each entry, following the same instructions as before.

If you'd like to go past the cotton mill, turn to **274**.

If you'd like to cut through the backstreets where the mill workers live, turn to **110**.

339

You fly forwards and tackle your opponent before he can draw his weapon. You were trained as an elite guard, skilled in hand-to-hand combat, and when your forearm connects with his chin you feel him go limp. You drag his body into the shadows.

Turn to **79**.

340

Trying to look confident, you stride towards the ticket office. One of the guards moves to bar your path and peers at you closely. A slow smile spreads across his face.

"Leaving town, are we?" he asks.

You nod, your heart sinking.

"Not today, you're not."

He motions to the others, and they close around you.

"To be honest, I expected better from a guard of your experience."

On your way back to the Citadel, Meg nuzzles your neck before slipping away undetected. It won't be long before the butler learns of your demise.

341

The butler invites you into the kitchen for a bite to eat before setting off.

If you accept, turn to **165**.

If you decline, turn to **380**.

342

You dare not hold the mirror up any longer, so you'll just have to hope you've spotted all those creatures in disguise. Heart thumping, you make your way towards the gateway. And you nearly reach it as well, before you feel a tap on the shoulder.

"Going somewhere, Seagrave?"

You spin around and meet a smile that's warm as ice. The top hats are moving through the crowd. Closing on you. Your hand flies to your sabre, but the combined force of their attack is too much, and you open your mouth in a silent scream. Quickly they carry you into a room in the Citadel, and that's where your adventure ends, back where it all began.

343

On the far side of the courtyard there's a passageway leading deeper into the Doldrums. Bare clotheslines stretch between the windows and it's so dark you nearly trip over the legs of a man slumped in a doorway. Suddenly, heavy drops of water rain down. You look up and see a fisher hanging from a clothesline, its green eyes almost glowing. And there are more on other lines, on window ledges – you've never seen so many in one place before. They follow you in silence, until you feel something brush the top of your head. You look up, and the green eyes are barely an inch from your own. Screeches fill the passageway.

Roll one DICE and add your SKILL level.

If your total is 8 or higher, turn to **227**.

If it's 7 or lower, turn to **125**.

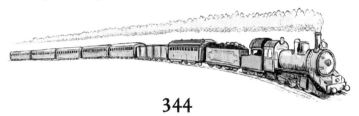

344

You shake your head, trying desperately to clear the memories flashing through your mind's eye. The man in the top hat sees his opportunity and lunges forwards. But there's a flash and a surge of heat from the pendant around your neck. He screams.

Make a note of the number of this entry (344).

Then, if this is the first time the pendant's been used, turn to **166**.

If it's the second time, turn to **314**.

Then, turn to **88**.

345

You rush down to the embankment and lob the smoke bomb at the monster's cavernous mouth.

If your SKILL level is 6 or higher, turn to **78**.

If it's 5 or lower, turn to **111**.

346

You step aside as the guard's limp body tumbles down the steps and into the water. Looking up, you see the third guard retreating back through the cottage. You've held them off for now!

Turn to **93**.

347

As you concentrate, the noise seems to fade. You forget to be scared and all you see is the ground ahead. The white peaks looming out of the storm. Deftly you spin the wheel one way then the other, knowing that a moment's hesitation could cost you your life. Until finally, slowly, the tempest starts to ease.

You feel a hand on your shoulder.

"It's alright, Seagrave. You can let go now."

You see Gambrel's face and remember where you are.

"Look!" he says with a smile.

Up ahead you see Demon's Well. The air is almost clear now, the sunlight breaking through. You stagger into the cabin and sit down, and Gambrel hands you a hot flask. As he returns to the helm, you notice his face is grave.

"The storm has damaged the engines," he says. "I can't land, or I might not get them started again. You'll have to drop from the ladder. I'll get you close. But there's a station at the bottom of the mountain for your return journey. Last stop on the line from Mirewick."

He laughs.

"If I'd known you were going here, I'd have told you to take the train anyway!"

As you approach the slopes of Demon's Well, he opens the hatch and lowers the ladder. Meg pokes her head out, then burrows straight back down again.

"Good luck, Seagrave!" Gambrel calls. "If you want to go on any more adventures, don't ask me!"

You clamber down until you're on the bottom rung, level with the trees. Below is soft snow. With a last look up, you let go.

Roll one DICE.

If you roll 1-4, turn to **298**.

If you roll 5-6, turn to **192**.

348

He slumps back against the railings. As you reach for the key, he grips your wrist, but the grip is weak and slowly he sinks to the floor and lies still. Glancing over your shoulder, you open the gates and slip through.

Turn to **76**.

349

You nod towards Blake and he nods back. The two of you have the skill and experience to know what to do. You spread out and advance, your heart thumping hard in your chest.

If Eldritch still has her staff, whenever you roll a double, you're hit by a lightning bolt, and must deduct 1 LIFE point regardless of whether you win or lose the round.

ELDRITCH

Rounds: 5   Damage: 2

YOU

♡ ♡ ♡ ♡ ♡ ♡ ♡ ♡ ♡ ♡ ♡ ♡

If you win, turn to **185**.

If you lose, turn to **233**.

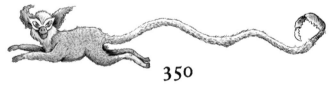

350

You sense she needs a little push to seal the deal. Clearing your throat, you rest your hand on the hilt of your night-sabre and say:

"You do have a permit to sell these items on the street, don't you?"

Her eyes narrow instantly, and you hold her gaze. After a pause, she holds out a leathery hand.

"Two shillings," she says.

Deduct 2 SHILLINGS and add the CLOAK to your LOG
BOOK. Then turn to **198**.

351

The ogre drives you back, smashing its club down left and right
until it catches you a heavy blow. You lie gasping in the snow as it
raises the club high. But suddenly there's a shout. It comes from Ivy.
She's being held by two imps, but they release her and she steps
forwards.

"Let the dreamless one go," she calls, her voice calmer now. "I
admit it! The fault was mine."

After a long pause, the old imp nods, and the ogre is dragged
away. You grab your sabre and scramble to your feet.

"Why did you come here?" she asks darkly.

Turn to **36**.

352

With the mirror still in hand, you look again at the pale river
flowing above your head. But closer this time. It's filled with
dreamlike images, and seems to be flowing towards the Citadel.
There's a galloping horse, a burning tree, a child's cradle, rocking.
But they're fainter now – the sky's turning grey and dawn is
approaching. You put the mirror back in your coat pocket and look
around. Details are starting to separate themselves from the night.
The wheel ruts on the cobbles, a little owl carved into the cellar door
by your feet. And above your head a pub sign creaks. Three Crowns

show dimly on the board, and suddenly you know exactly where you are. You think quickly. There are two routes to the Citadel that seem best.

If you'd like to go past the cotton mill, turn to **274**.

If you'd like to cut through the backstreets where the mill workers live, turn to **110**.

353

The cloak will hide your face, but would it attract suspicion? Might it be better to follow the crowd into the mill? You're out of time and must make a decision...

If you want to put on the cloak and try to walk past the guards, turn to **69**.

If you decide to follow the workers into the mill, turn to **372**.

354

It's the lightning that saves you – revealing the jagged peak that's waiting to tear a hole in your hull. Grabbing the handle, you turn the wheel hard to the right, over and over until the ship shudders and the engines groan. But somehow the rivets hold, and you clear the mountain with inches to spare.

Drawing a long, ragged breath, you level out and slowly take the ship back down. The blood thunders in your ears, all your senses heightened.

Turn to **347**.

355

Taking him by surprise, you snatch it from his grasp. His face goes red, but he forces a laugh for the crowd.

"Very good," he says. "Very good…"

And as he nods to himself, you see something you hadn't noticed before, beneath the swagger. Rage. He looks up.

"But officer, it wasn't very clever."

He launches himself at you before you have time to draw your sabre.

Turn to **101**.

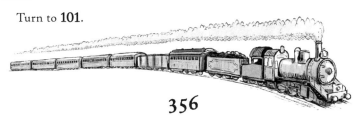

356

Further up you come to a small hollow. There are tracks running down the side, stopping behind a bush in the middle. They look like they were made by a child. Surely there's no one else this far out? Edging around the hollow, you see a small imp dressed in furs. She's got her back to you, and a white rabbit slung over her shoulder. She's busy replacing the snare.

You call out, and she jumps up as if she's been stung. But the strange thing is she doesn't turn around. Instead, she stands very still. The snow crunches underfoot as you approach. Something's not right. She looks over her shoulder and her eyes meet yours. And then she shuts them tight. It takes a moment to register, but you see a pair of green eyes painted on the lids. You say you didn't mean to make her jump, but she doesn't reply. You say you weren't expecting to see anyone out here and she turns to face you, the painted eyes staring.

"But you didn't see me, did you? There's no need to blab. It's just I'd never seen one before..."

She's got a flat nose and big pointy ears.

"Seen what?" you ask.

"One of the dreamless ones."

You ask what she means, but she starts backing away and tutting.

"So nosy! So nosy!"

Then she turns and runs.

If you want to follow her, turn to **241**.

If you'd rather not, turn to **129**.

357

You don't think they'll care, but there are procedures that must be followed. Questions to be answered. They can't just wave you past if you've fought with an escaped prisoner. So you just tell them she ran off, and ask to be let through to make your report to the warden. The second guard looks at the first, who nods reluctantly. They open the gates and let you pass.

Turn to **76**.

358

On the way back from the lamp, your foot slips as you're edging along the boat. Your hand comes down hard on a metal hook. Cursing your luck, you make the cabin just in time.

Deduct 1 LIFE point, then turn to **19**.

359

You can't keep him at bay much longer, your defences are weakening. And then you feel something small and furry climbing from your coat. Meg! She whips her hooked tail across the man's face, and as he cries out, his hold slips. In a single movement you draw your night-sabre and run him through. Gain 1 ABILITY point.

Gasping, shaking, you slump back in your seat. Your undershirt is soaked with sweat. The strange thing is, no one looking in would have known anything was the matter. The fight took place in complete silence. As your breathing slows, you look back down at the man's body. It takes a moment to realise what you're seeing – it's gone! The body's gone and all that's left is a steaming pile of clothes.

Turn to **388**.

360

You hold the looking glass to the light and the ice above seems to shift. The lines and shadows join with the cracks on the glass to form a picture, a face.

"Eldritch," you whisper.

Gain 1 ABILITY point, then turn to **211**.

361

It's been many days since you've tasted anything other than bread and water. You lift the bottle to your lips and take a swig, swill it around to savour the taste – and it's this that gives you time to feel the numbness spreading across your tongue. You spit the dark liquid onto the floor and poke the guard with your toe. He doesn't even stir. Whatever's in this bottle will keep him unconscious for a good while yet.

Deduct 1 ABILITY point and turn to **260**.

362

The second guard shakes his head when you tell them what happened.

"Sounds like Evie, alright," he sighs. "She had a dark side."

The first guard clears his throat.

"You'll have to wait here while someone comes to escort you to the warden. He'll want to question you."

You ask if they can just let you through to see the warden yourself, but he shakes his head.

"Not how it's done," he says.

Your heart sinks. You've no choice but to fight them.

Roll one DICE and add your SKILL level.

If your total is 8 or higher, turn to **379**.

If it's 7 or lower, turn to **267**.

363

You feel something warm and wet run down your back. Your opponent looks up, and your eyes follow. Teeth. Hooked and pointed and spiralling into foul, damp darkness. They fill your vision and close around you. The last thing you see is Meg, dropping through the gap before it closes. At least one of you made it out alive.

364

Your fingers curl around the smoke bomb. You wait until the town guards are moving through the crowd, checking the face of each prisoner they pass, and then you hurl it to the ground. The bang sends prisoners and guards diving for cover, and as the smoke spreads, someone cries out: "It's the invasion! The invasion!" The cry spreads through the prisoners like wildfire. One of the town guards shouts for quiet and they're hauled to the ground. Suddenly there are people running in all directions, stumbling through the smoke, and in the confusion you slip away and run the short distance to the woods.

Gain 1 ABILITY point, then turn to **44**.

365

One of Ada's gang comes up and whispers in her ear. She nods and grasps your hand.

"I have to go. Walkers on Colmore Row." She pauses. "What will you do now?"

You tell her you're looking for Eldritch and she frowns.

"You're the second person who's said that. There was a man. Strange one. Said he was from the prison on the hill. As a matter of fact..."

She rummages in her frock coat.

"Here, he gave me this. Told me to use it if I ever saw her."

She hands you a whistle that's cold and dark. A gold rune is carved in the side.

"Can't do you any harm, I suppose." She starts to walk away. "Oh, and Seagrave? Eldritch will be at the Field of Healing this morning at dawn. There's another execution. Don't know who, but she's never gone before. Must be someone important."

As she marches off into the night, you call your thanks and take a deep breath. So, you know now where all this will end, one way or the other. The place you've been running from all this time. The Field of Healing.

Add the WHISTLE to your LOG BOOK, then turn to **38**.

366

Ada rushes into the hold.

"I knew a guard would know how to aim!"

Leaning out, you see the hole in the guards' carriage, their ballista nowhere to be seen – you've blown it clear out the back.

You point questioningly at the crossbow. The next bolt has been loaded automatically.

"Silas built it," Ada explains. "He said I'd be grateful one day."

She trails off, then looks up.

"Come on. Let's go."

Turn to **197**.

367

The boy shows no interest in your offer.

If you want to threaten him, turn to **150**.

If you decide to climb back up to the courtyard, turn to **249**.

368

You make good progress, weaving through the crowd like an alley cat. Up ahead, you see a large peacock feather, bobbing over everyone's heads in the rain. As you get closer, you see it's sticking from an old lady's hat. She's pulling a handcart, piled high with odds and ends. A damp black cloak bundled at the back catches your eye. It might come in handy.

If you'd like to stop the old lady and buy the cloak, turn to **235**.

If you decide to just grab the cloak to save time, turn to **310**.

If you'd prefer to carry on your way, turn to **198**.

369

The bell rings as you enter the shop. The woman behind the counter looks over briefly before turning back to a customer. The place is warm, the windows steamed up. You smell the meat and gravy and see that a pie with a mug of tea costs 1 SHILLING.

If you have the money, turn to **24**.

If you don't, turn to **47**.

370

The old witch ghosts inside your desperate thrust and sinks her claws into your throat.

"There now," she says, helping you down to the floor. "Don't bleed too much – I was hoping to make pudding."

As the room goes dark, you hear Meg's desolate wail.

371

Your smile turns to a look of confusion as the spinner seems to slow suddenly, and comes to rest on the three.

Orson shakes his head sadly.

"I thought you had it then, I really did."

If you want to accuse him of cheating, turn to **195**.

If you want to play again, turn to **236**.

If you'd like to leave, turn to **53**.

372

Gain 1 ABILITY point. As you walk through the gates, you see cotton bales being unloaded from a wagon on the far side of the courtyard. A short, fat man is standing on a platform, watching the workers file past.

"Tie back that hair," he calls to a girl who can't be more than ten years old.

His voice is surprisingly thin.

"Tuck in your shirt, Jessop."

And then his eyes land on you. You can tell by the pause, even though you're staring at the wet cobbles.

"You there!" he cries.

You carry on walking.

"I said you there!"

You stop, and a circle forms quietly around you. The man jumps down and pushes his way through. He has a shiny bald head and thin spectacles perched on his nose. He looks up at you impatiently.

"What's a city guard doing walking through with the workers?"

"I wasn't sure where to go," you say. "I've got a message for the manager."

He sighs and looks around.

"Get moving!" he shouts. "Your shift starts in ten minutes!"

Then he gestures for you to follow.

"We'll talk in my office," he says.

Turn to **92**.

373

You haven't far to go. Following the towpath, you cross a bridge and enter a square with the station on the far side. Despite the north terminal being the quietest of Mirewick's stations, it's also the grandest. Huge columns guard the entrance, each one carved from pink granite – a rock found only in the Whistling Mountains. And in the middle of the square is a statue of Mayor Eldritch. It commemorates the opening of the line – a line that many people said could not be built, but which was finally completed at the cost of many lives. Eldritch is standing on a great slab of pink granite, one hand in the air and the other striking the rock with her umbrella. Cracks run from its tip, as if the slab is breaking apart under the weight of her stroke.

Crossing beneath her haughty gaze, you notice a group of guards standing outside the ticket office. They stop someone walking through and ask them to remove their hat and scarf before letting them past.

If your SIXTH SENSE level is 5 or higher, turn to **59**.

If it's 4 or lower, turn to **222**.

374

You shake your head. Slowly, you stand up and give Meg one last pet. The fire crackles and you want to apologise, but Arkwright holds up his hand.

"You have already saved Mirewick once."

Together, you walk down to the gates of Skerramore. Meg sits on his shoulder, just as she did when you first set out, all that time ago. In the distance, the evening sun catches the white tops of the mountains, and lamps are being lit in the smoky streets below. As he locks the gates behind you, the butler looks up.

"Goodbye, Seagrave," he says. "You may not remember us – but we will remember you."

So, with a last glance you walk away. And as your memories fade, just a lingering unease remains.

375

"Evie who?" the guard asks.

"Nightshade," the other replies.

"What did she look like?"

You say her face was painted black and white, and let impatience creep into your voice, as if you'd rather be somewhere else.

"So why didn't you bring her with you?"

You raise your eyebrows and the second guard chuckles.

"She was in the circus," he says. "Trapeze artist. Flighty little thing."

"What happened, then?" the other asks.

If you fought with her, turn to **138**.

If you didn't, turn to **223**.

376

You watch helplessly as the shreeker turns. And this time it makes straight for the balloon. It knows. There's a horrible tearing sound, and the ship lurches to the side. You see the ground far below, the vast marshes that will cushion your fall. But not nearly enough.

377

Your mouth hangs open as you struggle for an answer.

"What are you doing in here?" she says.

Her eyes flicker down, and you realise your hand is on the hilt of your night-sabre. She backs away, ready to call for help. And then you remember the card the butler gave you.

"Here!" you say, fishing it from your pocket, and apologising for the delay. "I'm here on business."

She relaxes slightly but doesn't move out of your way. There's something new in her expression, almost the hint of a smile.

"Still," she says. "There's something fishy here. I'll have to report it to the train manager. Unless..."

She leaves the sentence dangling, and you realise what she's saying. She doesn't believe your story for a second, but she's not interested, she just wants payment for turning a blind eye.

You can give her 2 SHILLINGS, or any item from your LOG BOOK except the NIGHT-SABRE or MIRROR.

If you choose to do so, turn to **276**.

If you'd rather jump off the train before it picks up too much speed, turn to **102**.

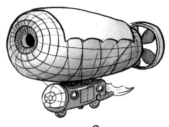

378

Except it's not a room. It's a path. You lie on the cold flagstones and hear the birds in the trees. Getting to your feet, you see Skerramore, and suddenly you're gripped by an urge to run. To catch a train or an airship and never look back. But whichever way you turn, the path leads to the old hall, and you realise you don't have a choice. Instinctively you reach for Meg, and realise she's not there. You're on your own. Slowly, you walk up to the doors and knock. There's no reply. You push hard and they creak open. The corridor is dark and empty, and your footsteps ring loud as you approach the great hall. But as you draw near, you hear the sound of a great wind, the splintering of wood and something beneath that. A wild, hollow groan. You pause for a moment, with your hands on the door, then you push. The wind and the noise force the breath from your lungs, and in front of you is a great, swirling void. You have to grab hold of the handle to stop yourself being sucked in.

"Seagrave!"

You hear a voice, small and clear, somehow cutting through the storm.

"Let go. It's the only way."

You look down and cry out. There, in the heart of the void, is a fiend. Like one of the creatures you've seen in the mirror, but stripped of all its disguises. And falling into its throat is the Watcher. She reaches up towards you and calls:

"It's Eldritch, Seagrave. But this is our chance! Grasp my hands to save us both."

Turn the page, and if you work out how to leap down to the Watcher, a pair of two-digit numbers will be revealed. Add them up and turn to that entry.

If you can't work out how to reach the Watcher, turn to **218**.

379

In one smooth movement you draw your night-sabre across the guard's neck. His hand flies up but it's too late for him. The second guard cries out and scrambles for his sabre.

PRISON GUARD

Rounds: 5 Damage: 1

YOU

If you win, turn to **348**.

If you lose, turn to **219**.

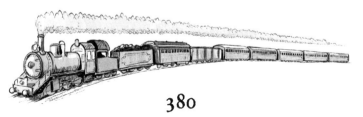

380

He sees you to the gates, and as you walk down the long driveway, Meg runs up and wraps herself around his neck like a scarf. You ask if he has any family.

"I see them on Sundays and special occasions, but the house is family too."

He glances back with pride.

"My son will follow after me. There's been an Arkwright at Skerramore for many generations."

As you approach the gates, he takes a card from his breast pocket.

"This will cover the cost of transport," he says. "Show this and they'll charge to my lady's account."

He hesitates and clears his throat.

"It's really very important that you reach Demon's Well... You're our only hope."

He opens the gates, and as you walk through, you feel something land on your shoulder.

"Meg?" the butler says.

She chatters gently by your ear.

"You want to go with Seagrave?"

She leaps back and nuzzles his cheek before returning to your shoulder.

"You're going to help, are you? Make sure everything goes off as it should?"

You tell him you're not sure if it's a good idea, but he shakes his head.

"She's made up her mind, I'm afraid. You're stuck with her now."

His tone softens.

"Just make sure you bring her back in one piece."

He smiles, and as you turn from the gates, Meg burrows down inside your coat. Beneath you lies Mirewick, smoke rising from its countless chimneys. Through the smog you can just make out a dark ridgeline on the horizon – the Whistling Mountains. There are two ways to get there: airship or train.

Add the CALLING CARD to your LOG BOOK.

Then, if you'd like to charter an airship, turn to **34**.

Or if you'd rather catch the train, turn to **136**.

381

Pulling back your sleeve, you load a bolt. Your best chance is to hit it from range, but you'll have to be quick, or you'll get hit yourself. Check your LOG BOOK and cross out any bolts needed to show the correct amount. Then...

... Roll one DICE.

Roll a 6: you kill it – fill in both halves of its crossbones.

Roll a 5: you wound it – fill in one half of its crossbones.

Roll a 1, 2, 3 or 4: you miss.

If your SKILL level is 5 or higher, add 1 to each roll. For example, a 3 becomes a 4.

After each roll, scribble out one of your remaining bolts below, then...

... Roll another DICE.

Roll an even number: the monster hits you – deduct 1 LIFE point.

Roll an odd number: you duck in time.

ROCK GHAST

If you kill the monster before running out of bolts, turn to **15**.

If you don't, turn to **291**.

382

The wind dies down as the trees close in, and your footsteps crunch through the dark forest. Climbing over a fallen tree, you stop. There's singing up ahead. The snatch of a tune, rising slowly and falling. Snow has started to fall, and you hurry on, hoping to catch whoever it is. The white flakes are swirling thick and fast, and you bury your hands in your pockets. Meg shivers under your coat and your feet are numb. Deduct 1 LIFE point.

Finally, you see a light ahead and smell woodsmoke. There's a small cottage in a clearing, and you see an old woman shuffling through the doorway, carrying a sack over her shoulder. She shuts the door behind her.

If you'd like to knock on the door and ask for shelter, turn to **269**.

If you'd prefer to carry on up the mountain, turn to **37**.

383

Your fingers close over the back railing, leaving your legs trailing across the sharp stones. Cursing, you scramble up onto the carriage.

Deduct 1 LIFE point, then turn to **184**.

384

You walk up to the cook with a confident stride and ask for a bowl of stew and a mug of tea. His small blue eyes are sunk deep in his fleshy face. He pulls a damp cloth from his shoulder and wipes his neck before ladling the stew into a bowl and pouring a mug of tea.

"That's a shilling," he says.

You point to your guard's badge and tell him you'll drop by with the money after your shift. He smiles, picks up the bowl and pours the contents back into the cauldron.

"I'll keep it warm for you," he says.

You grab the mug before he can pour that back too, and he shakes his head and mutters something uncomplimentary about the guards. You sit down at a table.

Turn to **167**.

385

Your heart beats heavy in your chest as you put your head down and cross to the other side of the street. The man's cry is lonely and sad. And then silence. You dare not look up. But perhaps this is what draws their attention. Who else would be so eager not to be seen?

"So, this is the famous Seagrave. Skulking past like a rat."

You freeze on the spot.

"I must say I'm surprised," the other says.

"Disappointed even," the first replies. "But what do you expect?"

"He's only human."

This last line they say together, and you hear a strange, rasping sound. They're laughing. Suddenly you feel that pressure again, probing inside your head, and you reach for your sabre.

"The Order will be maintained," they hiss, striding towards you.

If you lose a round, add together the damage ratings of both men, then take the total from your LIFE points. If one of them is dead, don't add their damage rating. If you win a round, deduct the COMBAT points only from the man you chose to attack. And remember to keep a note of how many rounds you have left for that man, too.

MAN IN TOP HAT

Rounds: 5   Damage: 2

YOU

MAN IN TOP HAT

Rounds: 5   Damage: 2

YOU

If you win, turn to **256**.

If you lose, turn to **301**.

386

You try to cramp the guard against the wall, but he sidesteps neatly and brings his sabre down hard. Your execution has come early.

387

Your voice gets faster as a grin spreads across his face. He doesn't believe you.

"Come outside," you say desperately. "I'll show you."

He scratches the dog's ears, and its lips draw back over its teeth.

"Look, I'm just waiting for an early delivery. That's why the cellar door was unlocked. My dad lives in the rooms above. If you come back at lunch, you can talk to him. That's when we open."

Deduct 1 ABILITY point.

If you want to threaten him, turn to **150**.

If you'd rather offer him a bribe, turn to **4**.

If you decide to climb back up to the courtyard, turn to **249**.

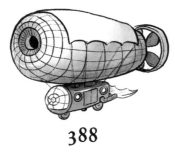

388

You lean across and lift the hat. The smell of brimstone fills the carriage, and you open the window. Cold, damp air rushes in like a splash of water to the face. What just happened? Suddenly, Meg starts chattering. She's been rooting through his clothing and tugs at something. A map. You open it out, and your breath catches. The train sways as you hold it closer to the lamp. Yes – there it is. A map of the Whistling Mountains, and a red cross, with '*Demon's Well?*' scrawled underneath. It's not far from the last stop on the line.

So, he was on his way to Demon's Well. Or where he thought it was, at least. You gather up his clothes and leave them to the dark pools of the Bottomless Marshes. Meg sits down beside you.

"We're on till the last stop, Meg," you say. "It's worth a try, at least."

Turn to **70**.

When you open your eyes everything's green and you're swooping through the air. The Watcher is back on her swing, the way you first saw her, and at the bottom of her arc she drops you onto the soft grass. You lie there panting as she swings above you, looking around the sun-dappled woodland. Finally, she comes to rest.

"You never know for sure," she says. "That's what makes it scary. I *thought* you'd do it, of course. But I didn't know."

You ask what she means.

"Find me in the dream-space. Where we needed to be to break her spell."

She sits down on the grass next to you.

"We haven't much time, so I'll be quick. Eldritch is weakened. In a moment you'll wake up back on the stage. Use the mirror again. Use it to reflect the light of the dawn into her eyes. Then the rest is up to you."

She grips your hand.

"And I'm sorry, because after that you'll have a choice."

You look down and see that her hand is changing. The shadows are stilled. The birdsong stops. And when you look up, it's like seeing a painting.

"My time is done now. I go on to whatever awaits. And I'm ready, after all these years."

She climbs back onto her swing.

"Rise and shine, Seagrave," she whispers.

Turn to **238**.

STEP-BY-STEP COMBAT EXAMPLE

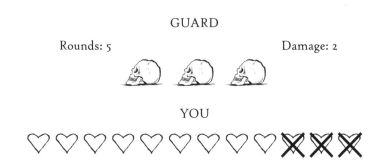

GUARD

Rounds: 5   Damage: 2

YOU

You have nine Life points, so before you start, you cross out three of the hearts to make nine.

Round one

You choose a Power attack and roll a 7. Your attack was unsuccessful. The guard inflicts 2 Life points of damage on you.

GUARD

Rounds: 5   Damage: 2

YOU

Round two

You choose a Standard attack and roll a 10. Your attack was successful. You deduct 1 Combat point from your opponent.

GUARD

Rounds: 5   Damage: 2

YOU

Round three

You choose a Power attack and roll a 5. Your attack was unsuccessful. The guard inflicts 2 Life points of damage on you.

GUARD

Rounds: 5   Damage: 2

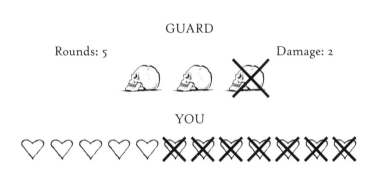

YOU

Round four

You only have two rounds left, so decide to try a Power attack again. This time, you roll a 9. Your attack was successful. You can deduct 3 Combat points, but only need to deduct 2 here. Your opponent has been defeated, and you can turn to the Victory paragraph.

GUARD

Rounds: 5   Damage: 2

YOU